THE GREEK BOY

by

Victor J. Banis

The Borgo Press
An Imprint of Wildside Press

MMVII

SECOND EDITION

◙ CONTENTS ◙

▲

◙ CHAPTER ONE ◙

It is funny, is it not, the way we hear different words or phrases? Take "boy," for instance: lots of people find that demeaning and would not care to be addressed in that manner; but from that first day I arrived in Kentucky I was "the boy," or, "the Greek boy." I guess I did mind, a little, anyway; but in time, I came to take pride in it. I still do, happily. But that came later; and I really do think I can say I earned that pride, and that happiness.

* * * * * * *

I had not expected Kentucky to be as green as it was. Not, of course, that I knew much about the place, only what I had read in the one book I could find in the library in Athens, which had been little enough, and what my mother had told me, which was not much more.

The Greece that I had left behind, probably forever, was beautiful in its own way, but stark, all white and gray and pink; a land of barren plains and jagged mountains that spilled down to that wine dark sea of legends. It is a land that goes back to our earliest myths, and touches us where we love and fear and hate—all our passions. Oedipus, Electra, Medea, Icarus. Surely there is nothing we experience in our lives that does not relate to one of those old tales.

Greece is like a man, hard, rocky, strong. These gently rolling hills of Kentucky, with the lush thick green that spilled over them and rivers that curled among them and seemed as if they had been painted there, were more like a woman, all curvy and soft, voluptuous. Only the sun was the same, hot and golden. It gilded the water of the river that followed the road upon which we traveled and caused the dust motes in the air of the bus to dance wildly.

I had spent weeks and several thousand miles to get here, and I had been all set to hate this place to which I had been, as I saw it, exiled. I had, in fact, worked overtime throughout the whole journey at keeping myself resentful and miserable.

That familiar sunlight, however, pouring through the window of this, the last bus in what had begun to seem like an endless string of them, chased all that misery and resentment right out of my mind, and I could only think how excited I was actually to be here, in Kentucky, America. I forgot my mother back in Greece, forgot my loneliness. I forgot everything but the wonder of the moment. I, Spiro Dimopolous, in America!

We had been driving along a curving, undulating highway, and now we had come into a town, the open fields giving way to neat rows of houses. The bus swayed and creaked around a bend, slowed, and wheezed to a stop. I swallowed nervously and I looked out at a dusty looking street, nearly empty just now in the midday heat. We had stopped directly in front of a drab looking building with a sign that read, Hardware; and beneath that, in smaller letters, Bus Depot.

"Rawley's Landing," the driver called over his shoulder as he got up from the driver's seat. He opened the front door and went down the steps and disappeared. The single other passenger, a silver-haired man in a well-worn jacket who had been sitting in the seat just behind the driver, got off too, leaving me sitting alone in my seat halfway back.

I was here at last, and suddenly I was frightened. I sat for long seconds listening to the tick of the overheated engine, and wishing I could...but no thoughts came to finish that wish. Wishing I could do what? I could not go back to

Greece. My mother had made that clear enough, even if the few dollars carefully folded together in my pocket had been sufficient for the return journey, as I was quite sure they would not be.

Like it or not, I had no choice but to collect my cheap fabric flight bag from the floor at my feet and make my way slowly down the aisle to the exit. Really, I suppose that flight bag was a falsehood of sorts: there had been no flights on airplanes for me throughout the entire journey, only a boat that really made good time but seemed to take forever, and busses that took forever but seemed to go fast.

I stepped into the bright sunshine and blinked, looking around and wondering if I actually would be met, as the single letter had promised. An old dog, so scrawny his ribs showed pathetically, sidled up to me furtively and sniffed about my shoes, wagging his tail timidly, but though I had an affinity for animals, I ignored him. He was not why I had come here.

There was someone waiting outside the hardware store bus stop and, since he had paid no attention to the driver or to the silver-haired gentleman when they had disembarked, and since I was the only other person to get off the bus, it seemed evident he was waiting for me.

He was looking away, at something across the street, when I first stepped down, so I had a moment to look him over and I had already sized him up by the time he looked my way and, surprised, saw me. I suppressed a little smile of recognition. Not that I had ever seen this particular individual before. I had not. But I had seen plenty of others much like him back in Athens, in Constitution Square. Throughout the whole long journey, I had thought with a homesick ache of all those men who paraded themselves in Constitution Square, around and around, or sat at the little café tables and watched the passing parade. In memory, I savored the almost endless flirting, the eyes that had looked me over with longing, and I had wondered if I would ever have a chance again to flirt back with men like that, to respond to that longing, or whether that, too, was now a part of my past, along with the square and the tables.

It was a surprise then, and a pleasant one, to have eyes once again gaze upon me with that familiar hunger in them, but unfortunately in that furtive way that so many non-Greek men had.

His expression was one of surprise, too. I do not know what he was expecting if not a homely little Greek peasant boy. Whatever the cause, his expression as he hurried toward me was both surprised and pleased, though I think I knew why they were pleased, seeing the quick glance downward. I had never gotten into the habit of wearing underwear, which had always made things simpler back in Constitution Square, and the loose cotton pants I had on showed pretty clearly what my handsomest features were.

"You must be Spiro," he said, smiling and offering his hand to me.

"Yes, I must be," I said, and gave his hand a rather over-strong squeeze that made him wince ever so slightly. It was not that I felt any distaste for his inclinations. Truth to tell, I probably was more "that way" than he was; but I had had ample practice at sizing up men; Greek men, certainly, but American men as well—by now, in nineteen fifty-five, the scars of the war had faded and the American tourists had begun to invade Greece again—and in my experience, this was what best turned American men on: a manner that was a little cool, even a shade insolent, but with still a hint of a promise in it. For some reason, that little bit of distance made them want you all the more and I was instinctively sure it would have the same effect on this man.

"Well," he said, and looked away from my searching eyes, a little unsure of himself. He rubbed his hands together—maybe I had squeezed a bit too hard—and glanced down at my solitary bag. "Are the others on the bus?" he asked.

"Others?" I said, momentarily confused. "Bags, you mean?" He nodded. I poked at the flight bag with one foot. "No, this is everything," I said, a bit defensively; but before he had time to register that, I asked, "Are you Branston?"

His eyes went wide and he laughed nervously. "Me? Good God, no, I'm Win. Winston. Winston Rawley. I should have introduced myself, forgive me."

"Are you my Uncle Winston?"

"Well, yes," he said with a faint smile. "I guess technically I am, but so many times removed, I can't even think what exactly you would call it. Third? Fourth? Anyway, I will feel a lot less ancient if we just make it plain old Winston, all right? Or, Win, that's what everyone else calls me."

"Okay," I said, showing off my familiarity with American slang, and smiled to put him a little more at ease. "Win it is." I reached down for my bag. He made a gesture as if to take it from me, but I lifted it quickly out of his reach. "It is all right, I have got it," I said.

He did not argue. It was obvious that I was stronger than he was, although the bag was not particularly heavy in any case. My meager possessions were not enough to make a bag heavy.

"This way," he said, walking a little ahead of me, but looking back often over his shoulder. He guided me around the combination hardware store and bus station. As a station, this one looked tiny indeed compared to the one in which I had gotten lost in New York City, but Rawley's Landing was only a village, of course, I knew that much at least. A town, I corrected myself. They called them towns here, not villages.

I glanced inside the station as we passed the open front door. There was a lunch counter in there, reminding me that I had not eaten since breakfast, early that morning. In Greece, lunch was rarely before two o'clock, and dinner never before nine in the evening at the earliest; ten was more likely, in fact. I had waited until I got here to have lunch, forgetting those early eating habits favored by Americans. That was something I would have to get used to. For now, though, it looked like I would have to wait until dinner to eat.

Walking behind Uncle—no, just plain Win, it was important that I fit in—I had the opportunity to study him a little more fully. If I had met him in Athens, I would have quickly guessed his English ancestry and his American upbringing; but I already knew all that, so my guesses here did not count.

He was good looking. He had been quite handsome once, I judged; but the looks had begun to fade the way they did with some men; especially with men who drank more than they ought, and I was willing to bet he did.

Well, he was homosexual, I was sure of that, and maybe guilty about that, the way middle-aged American men often seemed to be, in my limited experience. Probably he drank to forget and then, when he was drunk, did all those very things he was trying to forget. He was not the first man I had met with that kind of problem, one that Greek men did not often have, fortunately. Greek men tended to take it, and like it, where and how they found it. They were often reluctant to discuss it or even admit it, but that did not very often stop them from doing it.

He was still attractive though, and the drink had not yet taken its toll on the slim body under his linen suit. The suit had been white originally, and probably a very good one, but it was beginning to wear thin now and to turn yellow with age and too much dry cleaning. His ass beneath the aging linen was nicely shaped, though, and firm-looking, and I had already noticed an attractive bulge in the front of his trousers when he had come to greet me. It appeared that my new Uncle did not wear any underwear either. I felt fairly sure that it was not the only habit that we had in common either.

All things considered, the future looked a bit rosier than it had a few minutes ago on the bus. It was a comfort to know that there would be a Win around for the immediate future, with softly curved cheeks and an attractive bulge; and an eager gleam in his eye when he looked at my crotch.

He led the way to a motorcar in the parking lot, what the Americans called a "station wagon," a boxy shape with its sides covered in wood that, when I got a closer look, was not wood at all, but some kind of plastic or metal. He opened a door for me and I slid into the passenger seat and he closed the door and went around to the other side and got in behind the steering wheel.

"Sorry this isn't the most glamorous transportation," he said, taking off his hat and tossing it into the back seat;

his hair was yellow, too, like his suit, and also faded a bit. "But it runs good. That's the important thing."

"Is it new," I asked.

He laughed and said, "Not for many long years, I'm afraid." He started the motor and looked sideways at me. "I guess you don't see a lot of Chevys in Greece."

"Not many," I agreed. I wondered what he would think if I told him this would be my very first ride in a private automobile. The closest I had ever come before were busses. There were automobiles in Greece, of course. You had to dodge a sea of them just to cross the Constitution Square: government cars and taxis, all honking at once, and even plenty of privately owned ones, but I had never ridden in any of those.

I could see, when I looked around inside the station wagon—the Chevy, he had called it—that it obviously was not new. The upholstery was worn to a shine and the dashboard panel chipped; but I was still more impressed than I wanted to let on.

Rawley's Landing was a small town, smaller I judged than many of the villages near Athens. Win drove fast through the two or three blocks that made up the commercial district. There was not much to that: the bus depot, of course, and Willford's Fine Clothing across the street from it. The Eat Well Groceries was next to that, and Lederer's Hardware and Paints and Melanie's Flowers and Gifts, and something called a Dairy Queen. Past the business section, the street was lined with wide spreading trees, and beyond them big, old houses that sat discreet behind their white painted fences like retiring dowagers.

"That's our hospital," he said, pointing to a cement block building as we neared the edge of town. "Small, but surprisingly well equipped for a little town like ours."

Just a little beyond that, we passed a service station with a green dinosaur on its sign. That seemed to mark the end of town and after that we were back in the open country. I looked behind and noticed a sign as we drove onto the highway, and remembered what I had meant to ask since I had first heard of this place.

11

"The town is called Rawley's Landing," I said. "And the family is Rawley, too. Was it named for the family?"

"At one time the town *was* the family," he answered. "We owned it, all of it; every acre and every building. That was before the war, of course."

I thought about that for a moment. There were always wars, it seemed to me, and I was not entirely sure which one he meant. "The Second World War?" I asked. That was the most recent.

"Boy," he said with a chuckle, "You are in the South now, The American South. Which is say, The Confederacy and the union be damned. When folks here refer to the war, they generally mean the Civil War. The American Civil War. There are plenty of folks still fighting it, in their minds, at least."

"Oh." I remembered that I had read of that war, but not much, and it seemed to me like that had been a very long time ago; but I did not want to make a display of my ignorance. I looked out the window instead. We were driving now through that green countryside I had admired from the bus window. I looked at the fields on either side of the road and the wide leafed plants growing in them.

"Is that tobacco?" I asked.

"Yes." He sounded surprised. "Am I to understand you boned up on the lovely state of Kentucky before you came?"

"Boned?" I puzzled over the unfamiliar word.

"Studied. Sorry," he said. "Your English is so good, I forget you're not a native."

"My mother taught me, from the time I was a baby. We always spoke English at home," I said. "Was that the Ohio River in town?"

"No, that is the Cumberland. The Ohio is up north, on the border between Ohio and Kentucky, and the Mississippi is clear to the west. You'll probably see both of them sooner or later, though we don't do much traveling these days."

"I read that the grass was blue," I said, curious. This grass was green, though a vibrant shade of green in the afternoon sun, and not so dried out looking as it mostly was in Greece, where rainfall was scant.

"That's up around Lexington, the blue grass," he said, "In the central part of the state." As if he had read my thoughts, he added, "I guess this is probably a lot different than Greece."

"Yes, quite different." I turned to look at his profile and asked the question that I had been considering since I set out on my journey. "Is Branston the master?"

He laughed softly at my question, but it was not a mirthful laugh. "That depends on what you mean by master," he said. "He tells us when to shit. I guess you would call that the master."

We had been driving on a smoothly paved highway, but we turned off that now onto a narrow dirt road, not much more than a lane. He was still driving fast and the holes in the road made the car rock and bang. My head bumped against the roof of the car and I braced myself with one hand against the dash. He saw me and took the hint and slowed a little.

"Is he one of those people who does not like our kind?" I asked.

He got the intended hint and looked sideways at me, letting the car bounce through a bad hole with a noisy thunk. He concentrated on the road for a minute then, navigating around another rough spot, before he answered my question.

"Branston? No, he does not," he said. "Don't ask me what he actually does like, though. Pussy, I suppose. Personally, I have always imagined Branston fucking a rattlesnake, if he could find a snake would hold still for him."

He paused for a long moment, eyes carefully trained on the road, before he asked, "So, 'our kind' you said. Are you one of those Greek lovers you hear about?" He grinned when he said it, as if he were making a joke, just in case he had misunderstood my hint.

"Every Greek man is, somewhat; I think," I said, "Some more than others, of course." I deliberately stretched my legs out in front of me. The cheap cotton pants stretched tight across them and across the bulge of my crotch. It did not leave much to the imagination.

He glanced in that direction, and when he looked into my face again, his eyes were warmer. We regarded one another for a moment, smiling in recognition. He slowed the car and brought it to a stop right in the middle of the road, and leaned across the seat to me. One hand went straight for my crotch. I sat unmoving, neither withdrawing nor responding, while he felt me up.

"That is one enormous pecker," he said in an excited voice, giving it a hard squeeze. I did not know the word, but it was not difficult to guess the translation. He looked at my face briefly and when I seemed to have no objection, he fumbled with the zipper of my pants and got it open, and reached in. My cock strained up at him and he pulled it free. It was hard in an instant. It never took much encouragement. He slid his hand up and down the shaft, his eyes gleaming with excitement. My face was not handsome, I knew, but I knew too that my dick certainly was and I could see he felt the same about it. He leaned down across the seat and sucked the head of it into his mouth hungrily, making little slobbering noises.

It would not have taken more than a minute or two to bring me off, but he heard something and suddenly jerked away from me and looked out the windshield, down the road ahead of us. I looked too and saw another car in the distance, coming in our direction.

"Shit fire," he said and quickly started the car moving again. "Better put that away," he said regretfully. "We don't want to be seen fooling around like that."

I got myself tucked back into my pants, though it made a considerable tent of them. The other car passed by us and the man driving it waved, and Win nodded in reply.

"It's against the law here, understand, two fellows doing it together," he said. "Anyways, you're pretty young."

"I am eighteen," I said.

"That is still awful young," he said. "Getting caught messing around with you could put me in a lot of hot water, in more ways than one."

"Are you saying we are not going to 'mess around'?" I asked. That was a new expression for me too, and just as easy to translate as "pecker" had been. I was learning lots of new English, and it was far more interesting than what I had learned in school back in Greece.

14

"You bet we will, if you are agreeable," he said with a laugh. "That little taste I got of your pecker just gave me an appetite for more. We just have to be careful, is all. Jesus, never mind about the law, that ain't the worst of it. Let me tell you, if Branston ever found out we was sucking cock, there would be hell to pay. We mustn't ever let that happen. He would kill us both, that is for sure."

I was beginning to believe that Branston Rawley must surely be a monster. Which only made me all the more grateful to know that Win would be around, and available for "messing around." He was not exactly the stuff of a young man's dreams, but I was no beauty myself, and he was nice enough looking; and it had begun to look like he was all I would have to look forward to here in Kentucky, at least for the time being.

"This is Rawley land, from here on," he said out of the blue, waving a hand at the field we were passing. More tobacco, I saw, fields of it that seemed to go on forever, until they ran up against a distant stand of trees.

"All of this?" I said, awed. My mother and I, and my father when he was alive, had lived in two small rooms back in Athens, without even a blade of grass to call our own. Even with everything my mother had told me about her distant family, I had never realized that I was a relative, even a distant one, of anyone so wealthy. "The Rawleys must be rich indeed."

He gave his head a sad shake. "No, not any more," he said, "Not for a long time. I guess we were once, I don't exactly remember, that is so far back. These days, we manage, is all. Just barely, if you want to know the truth. Oh, from time to time we put on a show for the locals, but the fact is, the dirt is all we have left and the banks just about own that. That tobacco out there will see us through next year, if we are lucky. After that, who knows?"

I thought about that for a moment. If what he said were true, it made my position here even more tenuous than I had supposed. I suddenly saw that I could only be another burden for a family apparently already burdened. It was not the happiest of thoughts, and another one, even less happy, followed upon it. "He will not be glad to see me then, will he?" I asked. No need to say whom I meant. We both knew.

He hesitated for a moment before he answered. "Well, he invited you to come, didn't he? He didn't have to do that." We were both silent for a moment. His answer had not been much comfort. "Your mother is ill, as I understood it," he said.

"Yes," I said curtly. Uncle Win and I might be pecker-fondling friendly but we were not yet well enough acquainted that I wanted to discuss something that private with him.

If he noticed my abrupt coolness, he made no mention of it. "I got to say, I don't think I remembered her at all. Leticia, that is Branston's mother, she remembered her, so she says. They were cousins, distant ones, anyway. You understand, that sort of thing counts for something here. Cousins, uncles, nephews, they keep track of people they have never even met, just names. Anyway, your mother had visited sometime in the past, years ago. But then, she up and married the Greek—your father, I mean to say—and went to live with him in Greece, and that was the last we ever heard, until she wrote a couple of months back. I don't think anyone here even knew she had a boy till then. No offense."

"That is okay. I did not know anything about anybody here either. Just that Mama came from America. But she did not seem particularly American to me."

"You knew Americans, did you?" he asked.

"Some," I said, and let that fact go without explanation for the moment. Mostly, my acquaintance with American men had to do with all that cruising in Constitution Square but I thought it best not to get into that. "I guess by the time I was born my Mama had adapted to the Greek way of life. I never saw that we lived any different from any other Greek family. We were not any poorer, either, than most of the people around us. I guess we were better off than some. Papa owned a tobacco shop, which brought in enough for us to live on, or it did until he died. Then Mama got sick, and after a time, we lost the shop. I wanted to go to work and take care of us, but she got it in her head that I had to finish my education. That was when I learned that we had family here. I did not know anything about the Rawleys until then. Family is important to Greeks, too, though. Anyway, she wrote, to see if I could come here to live and finish my schooling, and, well, you know the rest. Only, I did not know things were as lean here as they are. I am surprised he let me come. Why do you think he did?"

He shrugged and said, "You never can know why Branston does anything. He just does, is all." After a moment, he added, "Never mind, he did, and you're here, ain't you?"

He reached across the seat again and gave my knee a squeeze, his hand lingering briefly, as if it wanted to travel up my leg a ways; but he thought better of it, and put his hand back on the steering wheel. "Don't let me scare you with my tales of hardship and want. You might get sick of the food after a while, but you won't starve, I guarantee that, and the house is clean and the beds comfortable. Only...." He hesitated.

"Only what?" I prompted him.

"That pride of yours," he said, "It sticks out like the horns on a bull. Pride is a luxury we Rawleys have had to do without of late, especially since Branston came back.

"Came back?" I echoed, surprised. "Was he not always here?"

"Branston? Oh, my, no, not since he was a boy, not till about two years ago. After Daddy died, Leticia tried running the place, but all she managed to do was run it into the ground, till it got so bad it looked like we were going to lose it all. That's when she swallowed her pride and wrote Branston. Not that she hadn't written him over the years; she had, apparently, but he had ignored her till then. For some reason, though, I don't even know if he answered her letter, in writing, I mean. He just showed up here one day out of the blue, looked us over like he thought we were some kind of lowlife. Truth to tell, I expect that is exactly what he did think. Anyway, he announced that he was here to put things back together so we would not disgrace him any further, the only hitch being that it was going to be his way, and no argument about it, and he has been the lord and master ever since."

"Could not someone just have stood up to him?" I asked.

"You haven't met Branston yet," he said with a humorless laugh. "If you had, you wouldn't ask that. Besides, there wasn't much of a choice, if we wanted to keep the place. None of us were up to running it, that was clear by then." He thought for a moment before he said, "To be honest, if it was up to me, I would as soon they had gone ahead and put the place up for auction. I would have gotten something out of that, small though it might have been. And I would not have to put up with that cold hearted bastard."

Watching his face while he said all this, I had no doubt of the depths of his hatred for his "lord and master." I could not help wondering what Branston Rawley had done to earn it. I was soon going to find out, too.

"This is it," he said, interrupting my thoughts. He turned into a lane that ran uphill. He stopped the car at the bottom of it and waved broadly with one hand.

I looked, and saw the house for the first time, at the top of the hill. It was more familiar to me than I could have guessed, an imitation Greek palace with tall columns and a sweeping verandah. It was stark white that gleamed in the sun so brightly it hurt the eyes and, like the farm itself, large and impressive. A lawn of lush green grass sloped downward toward the drive, past a small pond shaded by a tree with deep hanging foliage that almost touched the water, where a couple of ducks swam, iridescent blue in the sunlight. The drive cut neatly through the sloping lawn, flanked on either side by wood fences so white they too glittered in the sun.

"Everything is white," I said. That reminded me of Greece as well, where most of the houses were made of white stone, cheap and so much more plentiful than wood in that harsh land.

"Yes," he said, and seemed to notice for the first time. "Except for our virgin souls. Understand, we paint these fences here, the ones in front, where people see them. When you get around back of the house, you will find that the fences back there are unpainted. That should tell you something about the way we live, the Rawleys."

18

It should have, indeed, but for the moment I was too busy gawking at what was to be my new home and, despite Win's stories of hardship, I was mightily impressed by the grandeur before me. Impressed, and intimidated, I might as well confess. And frightened, as well, of how they would welcome me. Win did not count on that score. I had known from the first glance how he would welcome me, and in what way; but my fat Greek prick was not likely to count so much with anyone else.

In the weeks before I had left Greece, my mother had taught me as much as she could about American manners and customs, and I had come to understand that this new-old family lived on a grander scale than we had. I just had never dreamed how grand.

While I stared, Win had started up the car again. We followed the drive to where it made a little circle in front of the big steps that led up to the house. He parked there and got out, but I sat frozen as I had on the bus, staring.

He stuck his head back in the window, grinning as if he had read my every thought. "Might as well come on," he said. "No one is going to eat you. Least ways, not until I get you alone later." He winked and laughed.

I smiled back at him, grateful for his attempt to lighten the moment, and got out my side of the car, feeling all at once awkward and, what was worse, shabby. I stood indecisively, waiting, without knowing exactly what it was I was waiting for.

A woman, small and bird like, came out the front door and paused at the top of the steps. I was surprised to see her wring her hands together as she looked down at us. Being so nervous myself about meeting these people, it had not occurred to me that they might be nervous too. She looked friendly, though, and hardly threatening. She smiled down at me. I felt encouraged, and took a step toward her.

In the next moment, I froze as a man followed her out, the screen door banging violently in his wake. She jumped at the sound and seemed to forget me altogether, looking instead in his direction with a frightened expression.

"Branston," Win whispered beside me, but that was not necessary; I knew in an instant who this had to be.

19

From what Win had already had to say about him, I suppose I should have been frightened myself, and I guess I probably was after a second or so, but I might as well tell the truth: my first impression—my very first thought—was, what a magnificent lover he would be.

He was the Greek god of my boyish fantasies, come to life. Tall, imperiously so, divinely handsome; and, yes, like any God suddenly appearing before you, terrifying too. He had planted his booted feet wide. Legs encased in tight-fitting white trousers soared upward like the marble columns of the Parthenon, and the altar to which they led the eye certainly looked worthy of kneeling down to. The trousers were belted low on slim hips and his shirt, wet with sweat, clung to his massive chest. A sudden breeze teased his hair into a cloud of gold that framed a face carved from rock—and as cold and hard as any statue's. His eyes flashed with amethyst brilliance, like those of Zeus in the museum in Athens, so that you could easily believe he was about to cast one of those lightening bolts of his down upon you.

All of which is to say, he was one of those magnificent bastards that you hate at a glance, all the more so because the sight of them sets your balls on fire. I thought, for a moment, that I could smell smoke drifting upward from mine and I almost looked down to see.

Those amethyst eyes studied me with an expression I could not read, but I felt certain that he was judging me—and I was afraid they found me wanting. I do not know where I found the courage to climb those stairs, as afraid as I was. I did though, and I somehow managed to meet that intense gaze without flinching. Like him or not, I was this man's charity now. I was in those enormous hands of his, and not in the way that I would have wanted.

He was even taller than I had realized from below; two meters, maybe, so that when I was actually standing right before him, I was looking straight at that broad chest of his. A little tracery of sweaty hair showed where his shirt lay open. I forced my eyes away from that, and tilted my head to look up at him.

"So," he said, his face still expressionless, "You're the Greek urchin."

20

I felt my face burn red. Shame and resentment flared within me, and without thinking, I said, "So, you are the one who tells people when to shit."

It was stupid thing for me to do, of course. Not only had I gotten off on exactly the wrong footing with the one man upon whose charity I did indeed depend, but it was obvious that remark could only have come from one source, and Branston turned to glower down at Win.

"Bran," Win started to say, but Branston interrupted him coldly.

"Branston," he corrected him. "Call me Branston, Win, or, if you prefer, Sir. Never call me Bran."

Win clamped his lips tightly together, and Branston turned back to me. I thought for a brief instant that I saw something else in those eyes of his. I was not at all sure what it was, though. Curiosity? Or might it even have been a glint of amusement? Whatever it was, it was gone so swiftly that I was not any longer sure if I had seen it at all.

"My mother will see that you are settled in," he said. "If you want to get along here, you will have to get used to our schedules. And, yes, I set them. Including when to shit, I'm afraid."

I would like to have stood up to him, but neither my pride nor my anger gave me courage enough to face down this overpowering titan, and I had to drop my eyes from his. He glanced down at my pitiful little flight bag, and did not even, as Win had done, ask if there were more.

"Win will take that up," he said, and with that he was gone, down the steps and across the lawn, his strides long and free. I stared after him as he went. He was despicable, he was loathsome, he was vile.

He was all together virile, too; and the butt encased in those tight white trousers and moving so gracefully as he walked, was the most beautiful butt I had ever laid eyes on.

At the moment, I did not know which I wanted to do more: to kick it or to lick it.

THE GREEK BOY, BY VICTOR J. BANIS

◙ CHAPTER TWO ◙
▲

"So you're Antoinette's boy."

I had completely forgotten the woman standing beside me until she spoke and reminded me. I turned to look at her, trying, in my confusion over Branston, to remember her name: Leticia, was that it? Yes, Leticia. As I remembered it, I realized once again that she was nervous. I had been stewing about whether these people would or would not like me, but it had not crossed my mind that they might be having the same doubts. I saw doubt now, though, and her uncertainty, in the way she wrung her hands together and in the pleading note I heard in her voice. She smiled shyly at me, looking scared that I might not approve of her. Maybe—an idea popped into my thoughts, I do not know from where—maybe she was afraid that no one would ever approve of her.

"I am Spiro," I said, smiling to put her at ease, "And you are Branston's mother."

"Leticia," she said, and when she added, "Yes, I am Branston's mother," it sounded almost like an apology.

"That is the one thing, Leticia, I may never forgive you for," Win said. Now that Branston was gone, he mounted the steps nonchalantly and lifted my bag. "I'm going to stop in the kitchen first, for a glass of tea, and then I will just take this upstairs," he said. "Why don't you see that our young visitor here gets settled in comfortably, Leticia?"

He gave me a smile and, unseen by her, a wink, and added, "I am sure I will see you later."

"I hope so," I answered him, smiling back. He went into the house carrying my bag.

Leticia looked at him and back at me. "I hope Win hasn't been up to his old tricks," she said.

"Tricks?" I asked, all innocence.

She gave me a searching look and said, "You are certainly a sturdy looking young man." I was not sure if that statement was meant to clarify the earlier remark or not, and I continued to look innocent. "Antoinette was lovely, though, and I have no doubt she married a handsome man. He was handsome, wasn't he?"

"My father? Yes, he was surely," I said, and then added, "But then, I would think that, would I not?"

"Yes, I suppose," she said. "I certainly knew that my Daddy was the handsomest man in the whole world. Branston, on the other hand, loathed him. Not everybody loves their daddy. Not that Branston is anything to go by, of course. About anything."

She looked for a minute as if she were talking to herself, and I felt briefly like an intruder. With Branston there, it had been impossible to take notice of anyone else, but with him gone I could look more closely at her. She had been a beautiful woman once, I could see that, in a delicate way. She had an air about her like a piece of fine china, and just as fragile.

That beauty was long vanished, though. There was nothing left of it now but a ghost of what had once been. These Rawleys did not age so well, I thought. It was difficult to imagine that this bird of a woman had given birth to the godlike man who was her son.

She caught me staring and gave me a tremulous smile, as if she had read my thoughts. "I expect you are tired from your traveling," she said.

"It has been a long trip," I said noncommittally. I got the impression she wanted me to be tired, maybe because she was tired herself. I suspected she was generally tired, in all sorts of ways.

"I will show you your room," she said. "There's plenty of time to rest before dinner, if you want."

She turned toward the door and I hurried to open it for her, and earned another of her uncertain smiles. She led the way inside. After the glaring sunlight, the interior of the house was dark and cool, and smelled of damp and old stones and bricks. I could see that there was mildew in the corners.

It was elegant, though, for all that it had an air of shabbiness. The walls were wood below and paper above, some of the paper tattered and curling at the corners, and the ceilings were high. An enormous chandelier of crystal pendants caught what light there was and winked it back at us.

We had come into a large foyer. To the right, double doors were open on to a parlor the size of a hotel lobby, filled to overflowing with huge, old furniture covered in faded flowers. There was a fireplace black with soot and so big a man could walk into it upright. Musty looking velvet draperies that must once have been burgundy colored but were now a dusty rose hung at the big bay windows that overlooked the sweeping lawn outside. It was magnificent, and like the woman leading me toward the stairs on the opposite side of the foyer, an aged and wasted beauty.

The red-carpeted staircase spiraled gently upward, its wall lined with gold-framed portraits. "Be careful of the banister," she said, "The wood is old and rotten. Like the Rawleys, some might say."

Partway up, she paused and indicated one of the portraits on the wall. "That's my Daddy, there," she said. I paused briefly to look at him. He was posed in some sort of military uniform, one hand behind his back, legs spread wide, lips curled in a confident smile. Yes, she had been right, he was indeed a magnificent specimen of manhood. This was obviously where her son had gotten his looks.

Almost as an afterthought, she said, "That's Branston, there, next to him."

I was more interested in this one, and I took a good look. It was a very young Branston. The artist had painted him when he was no more, surely, than fourteen or fifteen, dressed in a hunting outfit: red coat, pale jodhpurs, black boots. He was standing alongside a nervous looking colt, holding the reins tightly in his hand.

Seeing father and son side by side, I thought Branston far and away the better looking of the two. He had his father's looks, true, but he had gotten something of her delicate beauty, too, and that had gilded the lily. He had long, almost womanly eyelashes, and lips so ripe and full that they looked already meant for kissing even as young as he was. He had also, at that tender age, already assumed the personality that I had encountered outside. If his father's expression was confident, the boy Branston's was arrogant to the point of contemptuous. He had developed into a bastard early, it seemed.

Leticia had hardly paused at all before Branston's portrait, and was already nearly at the top of the stairs. I had to hurry to catch up to her. We reached the first floor—second, I corrected myself, they called the ground floor the first floor here in America—and stepped into a different world. There was no pretense of splendor here, no show of elegance: no carpet on the bare wood floor, no furnishings along the empty hall, no drapes at the bare windows at either end. There was a single bare bulb in the ceiling where once another chandelier had obviously hung, but it was no longer there.

I must have shown my surprise. "It is just family comes up here," she said. "No point in showing off."

Her tone was bitter. I found myself thinking what an unhappy brood I had come to live with. And I would be here until I reached adulthood and had finished my education. I wondered if that bitterness would creep into me as well, the way a chill can, despite your best efforts to keep warm. I shivered at the thought.

She saw me shiver and misinterpreted. "Yes, it is cool here in the house. I assure you, however, you will find that welcome as the summer progresses. It gets hot here in Kentucky, but even in the hottest days of summer the house stays cool. Greece is hotter, though, isn't it, I suppose, so it probably will not bother you so much. Anyway, Daddy used to say he found it bearable so long as he had his bourbon and his poontang. God knows, he took to both prodigiously. This is bourbon country, Kentucky. Are you a bourbon drinker, young Mister Spiro?"

"I cannot say. I have never tried it," I answered her absentmindedly. I was thinking about that other word she had used: poontang. I made a mental note to ask Win, though I thought I could probably guess the meaning well enough.

She shrugged. "I expect you will like it when you have tried it. Rawleys generally do. The men, leastways. I never got much good from it myself. I always found I got drunk as well as miserable, never in place of. Here we are."

She indicated the open door of a bedroom. Unlike the other rooms we had passed, which had all been empty, this one had some furniture in it: a bed, at least, and a dresser. We had only had one bedroom at home in Greece, and the big front room which served as dining room and kitchen as well, and I had slept on a cot by the kitchen stove, so this seemed more than ample for me, but she seemed to think that it was a bit Spartan.

"It's not much, I am sorry to say," she said. "But the reason I picked this room for you is, this is where your dear mother slept when she was here. The bed is not the same one, I am afraid. That one was discarded long ago. This one came from my Mama's old bedroom, and the dresser was my Great Aunt Maggie's. She would be, let me think, your…oh, I don't know, I can't figure those things out anymore. I don't guess she would be much of anything to you, actually. Not that I suppose you care. Anyway, this is your room, and the closet is there, and you have got your own bathroom right here," she opened the door to show me that, "And there is this lovely little balcony, if you want to take some air."

The French doors to the balcony already stood open, sheer curtains of some gauzy material billowing faintly in the breeze. She stepped through them and I followed her out onto the balcony. It was warmer here, and the air was perfumed. I sniffed.

"Honeysuckle," she said. "And roses, but it is the honeysuckle you are smelling, it's lovely, isn't it. I know this must all be different for you, so far from your home and all, but if you keep your mind open, Kentucky can be beautiful indeed. Look there, you can see all the way to the river, the

Cumberland River, that is." She pointed to a distant ribbon of silver meandering through the green hills. "Although later in the summer, the leaves on the trees get too thick and you won't be able to see it."

She might have been talking to herself instead of me. There was a dreamy look in her eyes that said she had forgotten everything unpleasant for a moment or two, and was savoring sweeter memories. It made her look much younger.

She looked around and saw me, and came back to the present, her faraway look vanishing in a twinkling. "I hope you will be happy here with us," she said. "Don't let things…well, don't get dispirited, is what I wanted to say."

"I will not," I said, and gave her a genuine smile. "And I already do think Kentucky is beautiful."

She was pleased by that, but the faraway look came back. She stared out over the green lawns and the trees and the honeysuckle, and fluffed her hair with a nervous hand. "Daddy used to say that I was like Kentucky: beautiful, sweet, unspoiled." She smiled vaguely, but in a moment the smile was gone and she was a bitter old woman again.

"Oh, if only I were beautiful again, young Mister Spiro," she said in an anguished voice.

Something about the way she looked at me now made me even more uncomfortable than I had been with Branston, though in a different way I could not quite define. I was not frightened by her, as I was by him; but I think in some odd way I was frightened of her.

'I think you are still beautiful," I said, which was not quite the truth, but I wanted to comfort her. She looked so unhappy just then.

"Do you?" she asked eagerly, too eagerly, I thought, and she took a step toward me. I smelled her perfume, even over the scent of the honeysuckle, something cloying and too sweet and flowery, that she had applied with too heavy a hand. "Do you really think I am beautiful?" she asked.

She had fastened on that word, and I had the feeling that I had stepped onto treacherous ground with my offhanded compliment, but I could not think how to retreat gracefully.

She went past me, back into the bedroom, directly to the bed, and to my surprise, fell back across it, her pale yellow hair a contrast to the silver-gray of the comforter. "Come here," Mister Spiro," she said, reaching a hand toward me.

I felt trapped. I was a newcomer in this house and, more importantly, however much it might embarrass me, an object of charity, entirely dependent now upon the people who lived here. Clearly, I had already gotten off on a wrong footing with Branston Rawley, and I could not afford to offend still another member of the family. But even if she had been attractive to me, and she was not on several scores, my instincts told me that accepting her obvious invitation would be a dangerous mistake.

Nor was there any question in my mind of the nature of that invitation. Her breath was ragged, and her little breasts rose and fell rapidly. Her eyes glinted with growing excitement.

"Come closer, I say." Her tone was imperious, demanding obedience. She ran a tongue over her lips and said, "Am I really beautiful? Tell me again. I want to hear you say it."

I took a hesitant step toward the bed, unable to think what I should do. "Don't be frightened," she said. She reached for my hand, and guided it to her breast. Afraid to do otherwise, I squeezed it gently, making her gasp. I was surprised by its firmness. "How young you are, and already so manly," she said breathlessly. "Yes, feel my titty. I want to feel you, too. Let me."

She did, reaching for my crotch and fumbling at the outline of my cock. Despite my reluctance, it stiffened slightly at the touch. It had been many days since it had any attention but my own, and Win had already got the motor started a little while ago in the station wagon.

She ran a finger along its length, and sighed. "My, you are so big," she said. "Oh, take it out of your trousers, do, and let me see it. Let me taste it, too, won't you, you don't know how badly...."

She stopped suddenly, her fingers motionless, and looked past me. I looked over my shoulder to discover that

Win was standing in the open doorway, looking at us with an expression of distaste.

"I see you are introducing our guest to our quaint local customs, Leticia," he said dryly.

She scrambled hastily to her feet and smoothed the wrinkles out of her skirt. "How dare you come sneaking around on people," she snapped. "What do you want here anyway?"

"I brought Spiro's bag up," he said, indicating the flight bag in his hand. He looked past her to me and I flashed him a look of gratitude. "We eat dinner at eight," he said. "If you want a drink, that is before, in the library. There is plenty of time, though, if you want to take an afternoon nap. I believe that is the Greek custom."

"Yes, it is kind of you to suggest it," I said. I was not particularly sleepy but I was certainly glad for the rescue.

"I believe I will have a nap myself," Leticia said petulantly, and went toward the door. "I was only seeing that Spiro got all settled in comfortably, but it appears that you mean to take care of those details. Forgive me for mentioning it, Win, dear, but do remember that he is a guest, and a mere lad."

Win bowed low as she swept grandly past him and slammed the door after herself. He looked after her for a moment and then turned back to me. "Sorry if I interrupted anything," he said, and did not look it at all, "Maybe you wanted her to finish what she had started." he raised an eyebrow, making a question of it.

I shook my head. "No, not at all," I assured him. "I thought we already understood what my tastes are."

He took my bag to the closet. "Don't feel badly toward her. Leticia is all right, as a rule. It is just the scent of fresh meat invariably sets her off. We had to stop having delivery men come by. She couldn't keep her hands off a one of them, didn't matter a whit to her how old or how young they were, or how ugly, either, as long as they had a cock dangling, she was fit to get herself some of it."

He turned back to me and looked down at my still slightly swollen cock. "Of course, it's not hard to understand her enthusiasm, in your case."

30

Which sounded to me like a hint. I had gone far too long—not since a fortuitous experience with a cabin boy on the boat—without sex. That little episode in the car had started a fire to smoldering, and even Leticia's crude pawing had served to kindle it. Win was not exactly the stuff of dreams—he could hardly compete with Branston in that regard—but he was certainly not altogether unattractive either. And, the most important thing of all, he was here, and willing. Branston was neither.

And I was horny, very horny. I stripped my shirt over my head. My shoulders were broad and my chest and arms well muscled. Win watched wordlessly, but I saw his Adam's apple bob up and down nervously as I flexed my muscles, showing off.

I had more to show off, however, I undid my belt, slowly, to tease him, and then my trousers, and let them drop to the floor, stepping naked out of them. I knew I was a homely boy. My mother had told me so herself many times, but I had seen desire in the eyes of more than a few men already, and always when they got to see me naked. I was dark skinned, with my mother's bright green eyes and my father's jet-black hair spilling over my forehead in wayward curls. I had the short, sturdy build typical of young Greek men—and, best of all, the long, fat Greek cock as well.

Which for many men over the years had made up for my lack of good looks, and I could see it did too so far as Win was concerned. He stared wide-eyed at it, chewing his lip, while it grew, all on its own, longer and fatter. That was a trick I had, which never failed to impress—I could get it hard without ever touching it.

This time it was I who fell back across the bed, my cock by now standing proudly erect for his contemplation. I let him feast his eyes.

"Do you not want to join me?" I asked him in a teasing voice. His cock—what had he called it, a pecker—his pecker was already making the answer obvious, but he looked anxiously toward the door even as he began to unbutton his shirt.

"If anybody was to catch us," he said, kicking off his trousers. "There would be trouble, and plenty of it."

"Does not the door lock?" I asked pointedly.

"Well, yes it does," he said. He went to it. There was a key already in the lock, and he turned it with a click. "There, that's safer," he said, and paused. "Only, if anyone comes, they would wonder why it was locked, wouldn't they?"

"Do they not take naps?" I asked. "Leticia said just now that she was going take one."

"Branston don't. Branston never hardly seems to rest at all." He thought for a moment. "But he is working outside just at the moment. Let's hope he stays there. Anyway, now that I consider, I don't imagine he would be coming to look in on you. He is not the hospitable sort, as you may have noticed."

His decision made, he peeled off the rest of his clothes and dropped beside me on the bed. His pale skin looked like snow beside mine, and he smelt of stale tobacco and whiskey; but the cock that pressed against my thigh was rock hard and well sized, and when I ran a hand over his buttocks they were smooth and still firm. I ran a finger down the damp crevice and pushed a finger inside him. The muscle there gave my finger a welcome squeeze. It had been used, I judged, but it was far from used up.

He moved as if he meant to kiss me but I put a hand behind his head and pushed it meaningfully downward. I was not much for kissing in these situations. This was not romance, only sex. He got the message. He kissed my chest instead, flicking a tongue briefly about each of my nipples, and his hand reached down, his fingers toying briefly with my thick dark bush, and took hold of my cock.

"Jesus, you are really something," he whispered, raising his head to look at what he held. "No wonder Leticia's pussy got all wet.

He lowered his head and sucked it into his mouth, making a shudder of pleasure dart through me. I liked sex in just about all its variations, at least man on man sex, but I think there are not many things any nicer than having your cock sucked royally. I pushed upward with my hips, shoving it down his throat. He swallowed briefly on the sheer length of it, and then quickly began to suck gratefully and expertly.

He might be isolated out here on this farm, but Win had certainly managed to stay in practice. I wondered idly how. That suggested that he and I were not the only two of our kind in the neighborhood. I would have to ask him about that in the future. For now, though, there were other matters to deal with.

While he ate me with considerable skill, he fondled my balls, rolling them gently in his hand. He was mostly turned opposite of me and I was still fingering his butt, so that his cock was in front of my face. Well, what the hell, I thought, turnabout is fair play, is it not, and a hot, tasty dick was just about my favorite food. I put my tongue out and licked away a little pearl of come from the tip of its head, and he wriggled excitedly and pushed toward me. I opened my mouth obligingly and took him, my lips slipping up and down, savoring the sweet, salty taste. It seemed as if he must have done without such attention for ages, as excited as he got. We quickly fell into a rhythm, face fucking together with increasing speed and fervor.

The pressure in my balls began to grow quickly. I was too horny to prolong things and my orgasm was fast approaching. I sucked harder and shoved myself mercilessly down his throat, which only got him even hotter. His ass began to jerk and twitch and he lost his rhythm, suddenly swelling in my throat, and then it burst, and began to spit a white-hot stream into my mouth. I swallowed hard and fast, fucking his mouth for all I was worth, and in another second he was hungrily gobbling down my own flood.

We lay for a while without moving, savoring the afterglow of satisfying sex. He ran his hands over the cheeks of my butt and felt gently at my hole. "I tell you, I would truly like to get into that," he said.

I laughed and gave his backside a gentle swat. "Sorry, you can feel it all you want, or tongue it if that is your pleasure, but your tongue is all you will get into it. That is one thing I have never done."

He sat up surprised and looked into my face. "You have never done it at all?" he asked.

I shook my head. "Not even once," I said.

"Well, how do you know that you won't enjoy it, then, if you have never even tried it?" he asked. "Once they get a dick up there, a lot of fellows find they like it mighty well."

"I probably would like it," I said and shrugged. "I truly enjoy the feel of a hot tongue up there whenever anyone has had a mind to do that, so I expect a dick would feel good too, once it got things worked loose a bit."

"Well, then, what is the problem?" he insisted. "I assure you I would be most happy to demonstrate for you how pleasant it can be."

I sat up against the headboard and shook my head again. "I always dreamed that one day I would meet someone different from the others," I said, "Someone really special. And I thought that if Mister Right ever did come along, it would be great to have something that I had saved just for him, like a special offering, if you understand what I mean."

"You mean nobody is ever going to poke that pretty little ass for you?" He seemed quite unbelieving.

"Not until Mister Right."

"Well, it surely is a shame," he said, with a sigh, "Letting a sweet little piece of tail like that go to waste, and no telling if this Mister Right is ever going to show up."

I put my hands behind my head and smiled up at the ceiling. I was not going to tell him that I already knew who I wanted to give my little treasure to. For certain he would have thought I was crazy as anything.

Besides, even if he learned about it, it did not seem like there was the slightest chance that Branston Rawley would have any interest in what I had been saving all these years for him, since before I had ever laid eyes upon him.

It was his, though. I knew that for certain. Whether he wanted it or not, now that I had set eyes on him, I could not imagine giving it to anyone else. So maybe Win was right—maybe no one was ever going to poke it.

I could still dream, though, and it was Branston of whom I would dream hereafter, and no one else.

* * * * * * *

When Win had gone, and my physical wants had been taken care of for the time being, I put on my trousers again and stepped shirtless out onto the little balcony. The sun was dropping toward the horizon beyond the Cumberland River, painting the distant clouds pink and yellow, like a ripe peach, so that I felt like I could reach out and take a piece and bite into it. The flowery scent—honeysuckle, I remembered she had called it—was even stronger than before and in the distance I could see the glint of sunlight on water. It was peaceful here, and quiet, and I thought after all that perhaps it would not be an unpleasant place to live, even though I was a bit homesick. But home, that home, was a long distance away now, and this was where I was. Sometimes you had to make do with what you had.

A movement below caught my eye and I looked down. From here I could see the various farm buildings: an enormous barn, assorted sheds, a pen in which I could see several pigs lolling in the mud, a small stone house almost hidden by trees.

A door had swung open in the side of the barn and as I watched, Branston Rawley stepped out and closed it carefully behind himself. Even at this distance, looking down on him from above, his size was impressive. Everything about him, in fact, was impressive. I had more than a passing acquaintance with men's bodies, and I could generally tell in a glance or two how skilled or how clumsy they might be when it came to using them for sex, and so far I could say in all modesty that I had never been wrong. Branston walked with a loose-hipped gait that said, practically shouted, that this was a man who knew how to fuck, and fuck right.

I stared down at him as he came across the barnyard toward the house, and even though I had shot a load just a few minutes earlier, I felt a familiar heat spread through my crotch and my dick made a bid for my attention.

In my mind, I stripped his magnificent body naked, and imagined it sprawled atop me, those thick muscled arms crushing me to him. Some god must have been making mischief when he gave a man who was so obviously straight those lips so full and ripe, so perfectly suited for sucking cock. I imagined them clamped tightly around my cock, and it grew still bigger in my trousers.

I was thinking so hard about him, and getting so hard while I did it, that it almost seemed as if he heard my thoughts. He stopped abruptly and looked straight up at me as if I had called his name. I knew perfectly well that he could not see my hard-on, hidden as it was behind the railing of the balcony, but I blushed anyway, for my erotic fantasies. I was half afraid he would read in my face. Nevertheless, though, I could not look away from those piercing eyes that now regarded me steadily.

"It's Spiro, is it?" He said it wrong, as if it were "eye," not "eee."

I corrected him: "Spear-row," I said, which I immediately thought was probably a mistake. I doubted that he would like being corrected.

"Funny name," he said, and went on his way, disappearing from view.

My face burned. I went in and slammed the balcony door behind me, the fragile glass panes rattling in protest. What was so damned funny about my name, I wondered? It might be unusual here, but Spiro was about as common a name as you could find in Greece. For that matter, what kind of a name was Branston? Bran, Win had called him. If I remembered my English, that was a kind of grain, was it not, or a cereal? How would he like it, I wondered, if I started calling him Oatmeal? Or Wheat Flakes?

I threw myself on the bed again, frustrated, and looked around the sparsely furnished room. There was no use in wishing for what could not be. Like it or not, this was my home now, this big, strange mansion in this unfamiliar land. The life that I had known was far behind me. What kind of life awaited me here, with a dotty old woman and a fading, hot-pants homo—and that splendid but mean spirited bastard to keep me horny and angry all at the same time?

◉ CHAPTER THREE ◉
▲

I woke two hours later, surprised to discover that I had, after all, fallen asleep. To my dismay, I had not taken off my trousers and they were now badly wrinkled. I only had one other pair, carefully rolled in my bag. I took them out and put them on. I would need more than these two pair, I supposed, but I doubted if the small sum of money I had left would buy them. Of course, I could tell my new benefactor, and perhaps he would deign to add to my limited wardrobe; but, at best, it would give him another opportunity to gloat over my inferior status. I decided I would rather go naked, if it came to that.

I looked at the clock by my bed. It was more than an hour till dinnertime, and I remembered that I was expected to be punctual. I went down the stairs, seeing no one, and let myself out the front door. Everything was quiet. I sat on the front steps and looked out over the lush grounds, noting how well kept they were.

A noise behind me caused me to start and look over my shoulder. Win had come out the front door. He sat down beside me and gave me a companionable smile. "A penny for your thoughts," he said. When I looked puzzled by the unfamiliar expression, he said, "It just means you looked deep in thought. I was wondering what it was that had you so far away?"

"Everything is so well kept up, I said, nodding, "I was just wondering where all the help is that works the place."

"He's inside," he said, "Washing up for dinner."

"He? You mean Branston? He is all the help there is?" I asked, surprised.

"He is, except for what I do, which I will readily admit is little enough. The women see to the house, of course, but outside is his province. Of course, he will have you to help him now. Don't think he won't expect it, either. He will."

"I expect it too. I can work," I said, "And I will. I mean to earn my keep. Still, it must be a lot for him to take care of, this whole big place."

"There is a lot of Branston," he said, and though his dislike for the man was evident in his voice, I was suddenly aware of something else, too: I was not the only one who realized what a desirable specimen of manhood Branston Rawley was. Win might hate him passionately, but he would happily have knelt before the altar of that bulging crotch, at the slightest invitation.

Of course, I knew as well as he must that he would never get that invitation. Branston was not the man-on-man type; and even if he had been, as I could not help but fantasize, I was pretty certain Win would not have been the man he got on. He would certainly expect something far more splendid, more worthy—more like himself, was what it came down to. Not Win, surely. And not, sadly, me either. I was just another mortal, and not even the best example of that species, either. Mere men might enjoy my body—many had—but it was hardly suitable for a god.

Somewhere inside the house, a clock struck the hour. "Speaking of washing up for dinner," Win said, standing and brushing off his trousers, "We had best do that too. Meals here are punctual."

"More of Branston's rules?" I got up as well.

"You had best get used to them," he said. "He don't take kindly to having them flouted."

* * * * * * *

I went back upstairs to my room and washed up before I came down, and combed my hair as best I could, though as usual it ignored my efforts and tumbled in curls about my face where it chose.

No one had pointed out to me where the library was, but it was easy enough to follow the sound of voices down the hallway. I went through the open door and paused just inside the room. Branston sat in a big winged chair facing the door, so he was the first one I saw, and the first who saw me. He gave me a look that was surprised and, quickly turned to anger, his hard eyes looking me up and down coldly.

I knew why in an instant. In place of the tight trousers and the open shirt he had worn earlier, he had on a crisp white linen suit, with a pale blue shirt and a yellow tie. He looked every inch the country gentleman, as handsome dressed up as he was in working gear.

I stared around the room. Leticia's green silk dress was floor length, and looked quite formal. There was another woman in the room, only a little older than I was, and though her lilac colored gown was shorter, it too looked "dressed-up."

Win stood frozen in the act of pouring a drink and stared with the others. He was wearing a jacket and tie as well. *You might have warned me*, I thought, giving him a resentful glance. Though, really, I did not know what good that might have done. Shabby as my plain cotton pants and pullover shirt were, they were the best I had.

"Don't you have a coat and tie, boy?" Branston asked in that icy voice of his, which made me feel even worse than I did already. My face turned beet red and I could only shake my head mutely in answer.

"Get him a tie, Win," he said, not even looking in Win's direction. I would have followed Win out of the room, but the master was not having that. He gave an imperious wave of his hand and said, "Sit down, boy. Win will bring it here."

I did as he ordered. I sat in the nearest chair, biting my lip and staring straight ahead of me. I hated everyone. Him, most of all, for the way he had spoken; and Leticia, because she so obviously pitied me, and the other girl because she looked both amused and curious; and Win, because he had not warned me, or stood up for me.

Most of all, I hated myself for being a being a poor relation and having no choice but to suffer his humiliation. I wished I were dead. I wished Branston Rawley were dead too, needless to say. After I had fucked him to death, of course.

Win was back in minutes, though they had been an eternity to me. I stood up again and he handed me a gray necktie and gave me an anxious look the others could not see.

"Put it on," Branston said, as coldly as before.

I had never even owned a tie before, let alone tied one. I draped it around my neck and stared at the two ends helplessly. My eyes blurred with tears of frustration and shame. I tried helplessly to tie it into a knot, but the ends refused to cooperate.

"I do not know how," I finally had to admit shame-facedly.

"Have you never tied a tie, boy?" Branston asked.

"No, I have not," I said. I made a stab at standing up to him. "And the name is Spiro, sir. Spee-row."

If he resented my little rebellion—or even noticed it—he gave no sign. "Show him how, Win," he said.

Wordlessly, Win obeyed the master's command. He avoided looking directly at me while he tied a neat knot and tugged it up to my throat, and stepped aside for Branston to see.

"Fine," Branston said. "Now, take it off, boy, and you tie it."

Of course, I should have watched what Win did with it; I might have known I would not get off that easily. I tried, but the results were a far cry from what Win had done. Without a word, Branston signaled for Win to do it again. I watched closely this time, and when he had finished, I undid it and tied it again without being told. It was not that I wanted to please that goddamned man sitting in the chair watching me, but I did not want to give him the pleasure of thinking that I was stupid as well as poor.

The result was far from perfect, but it seemed to be acceptable. "Well done," Win said. "Maybe I should give Spiro a drink to celebrate the lesson he's learned."

Spiro has learned more than one lesson tonight, I wanted to say, but I kept my thoughts to myself. I did not get the drink, either, though by this time I would have welcomed one.

"It's eight o'clock," Branston said; unnecessarily, since the hall clock chimed the hour even as he said it. "In case no one has told you, boy, we eat dinner at eight o'clock. Sharp." He stood and offered Leticia his arm, and nodded toward the younger woman. "This here is Ellen, Win's daughter," he said.

It had not occurred to me that cock-hungry Win might have fathered a child. Branston must have seen my surprise. For a second or two, something that might almost have been a smile hovered about those voluptuous lips. But surely I had only imagined that.

"Yes, Win is a daddy," he said. "Of course, I expect he spit it in."

"You might show my wife some respect," Win said. "She is dead, after all. The dead deserve respect, don't they?"

"She was white trash," Branston said, unmoved. "The commonest kind, Leticia." Leticia took his arm as meekly as if they had only been discussing the weather, and the two of them started together toward the dining room.

"You are such an asshole," Ellen said as they went past her.

I was astonished to hear anyone stand up to him, but he remained entirely unruffled by her disdain. "Trash breeds trash," he said, not even deigning to look at her. "Boy, you can escort Ellen to the dining room."

I was so completely cowed by the man that I actually would have done as instructed, but Ellen gave me a frosty look when I held my hand out to her and went quickly past me into the dining room behind Branson and Leticia. I glanced at Win, but he shrugged and followed her, leaving me to bring up the rear.

The dining room was filled with more of the same once elegant but now sadly worn furnishings. When we were seated at the big old mahogany dining table, a grim-faced woman came through the swinging door from the kitchen and set a platter of roast pork on the table next to Branston.

"Mrs. Corey," Leticia said as the woman disappeared back into the kitchen. "She comes days to cook and clean. I'm sure Branston would as leave dispense with her meager services, but one taste of my cooking put quit to that."

"Leticia's wifely skills were all of a particular sort," Branston said, carving the pork into neat slices and piling them on a platter, which he passed to Leticia after serving himself.

Leticia looked about to reply, but Mrs. Corey came back with a bowl of plain boiled potatoes and another of some greens with bits of bacon in them. It was a simple meal, but the food was good, and I was ravenous, having missed lunch.

Nevertheless, I remembered what Win had told me about the family's finances and, since I wanted no more of the master's temper, I helped myself to just one slice of meat and a single potato, with a dollop of the greens. Surely no one could begrudge me that much, I thought. When the platter came back to me a second time, I shook my head and went to pass it on.

"You want to eat, boy," Branston said. "It's not fancy, I know, but it is the best we can do."

"I am not used to fancy food," I said, with no more than the merest suggestion of sarcasm in my voice. "And I do not want to be a unnecessary expense."

"Meat and potatoes are less expensive than nursing a sick Greek," he said.

I took two slices of the pork, and some potatoes, and a huge serving of the greens when they came back around; but I had lost my appetite, and got them all down only with difficulty.

* * * * * * *

42

The sun was barely over the horizon the next morning when I was awakened by a knock on my door and Ellen put her head inside to announce, "Breakfast in fifteen minutes. You won't want to be late. Latecomers don't eat. The master's decree."

She smiled when she said it, which made me realize that she was far prettier than I had thought the night before, with her sullen manner. I smiled back, and held the sheet up to my chin to conceal my morning erection, but she was gone already without taking any notice of it.

I was determined that I would make no more mistakes with Branston. I was dressed and downstairs in just over ten minutes, even allowing for tying the necktie three times before I got it right.

Which, as it turned out, was another mistake. The first thing I saw when I came into the dining room was that Branston was in his work clothes, the boots and open blouse and the tight white trousers of the day before.

"I will go change, sir," I said, frozen in the doorway and embarrassed all over again. "It will only take me a minute."

"Sit down and eat breakfast," he said, barely glancing at me.

I was surprised at the quantities of food Mrs. Corey served to this "poor" family. There were sausage patties with white gravy on them and more potatoes, this time browned and crisp, and eggs fried in butter, and all of that accompanied by hot rolls, which Leticia told me were called biscuits, which I thought meant cookies, and a large bowl of butter kept cool in ice, and a jar of honey.

Breakfast in Greece meant coffee and a roll, and it came much later in the morning, never before nine or ten o'clock. This was early for me, and I settled for a couple of those delicious rolls—biscuits—slathered with butter and honey.

"Why, surely that is not all you mean to eat?" Leticia said, almost the first words she had spoken. They were all of them quiet, in fact, concentrating on the food on their plates. I looked across the table at her and then, quickly, to Branston, who gave me a measuring look back.

"Best learn to eat when it is set before you, boy," he said. "It is foolish to waste good food, and farming is hungry-making work."

I put eggs and potatoes and sausage on my plate and went diligently to work on them, glancing in his direction from time to time to see if he was satisfied, but after that one brief comment, he was content to ignore me. I was relieved and disappointed all at the same time. He was certainly the most aggravating man in the entire world. He was right, though, it was good food, and once I had begun I found I had no difficulty in cleaning my plate.

He ate more than I would have imagined three men consuming, eating with a single-minded determination that made me wonder if his other appetites were as voracious. His plate emptied, he stood up abruptly. "I will beg your leave," he said gruffly, nodding in Leticia's direction, and strode imperiously from the room. When he had vanished there was a noticeable lessening of tension about the table.

I had expected to be put to work right off, but it seemed that there were other plans for me. "You have a real treat in store for you today," Leticia said, smiling playfully at me. "Win is going to take you into town." I looked surprised at her, and puzzled, too. "To do some shopping," she added in the way of explanation.

I tried to hide my excitement but I could not help the grin that spread across my face when I looked at Win, and wondered how on earth he had managed to arrange that with the master.

He and I went shortly after breakfast. There was another car in the garage alongside the station wagon, a black one that must have been a city block long and looked fit for royalty. "Is that ours, too?" I asked, gaping at the polished finish and the shining chrome.

"The Caddy? Yes, that is the royal chariot," he said dryly.

Clearly, we were not royal enough, however. We went in the old station wagon as before. "I suppose Branston drives that one," I said, indicating the Caddy.

"That is for state occasions," he said, backing the wagon out of the garage. "Branston generally drives the pickup truck. Or the tractor."

The pickup truck was parked outside the barn. It looked old and over-used, with one black door that looked newer than the rest of it, which might once have been green or blue, but had long since faded to a patchy non-color, with here and there a bit of rust for decoration.

It surprised me that Branston would choose that for his transportation, when obviously there were more comfortable options available to him.

* * * * * * *

Rawley's Landing had a minimal shopping section, that single block on the main street downtown, where the bus depot was. We parked in the same lot as before, next to the depot. No one had said what it was we were shopping for, but I had guessed that we had come to supplant my meager wardrobe.

My guess proved right. Win led the way across the street to Willford's Fine Clothing, a modest but tidy looking clothing store. I was overcome with gratitude toward Win for his thoughtfulness and his generosity. I felt certain that he was trying to make up for all the embarrassment that Branston had caused me—and, too, help spare me any more. I made up my mind that I would show my gratitude at the first opportunity. I had no money, of course, but there were other things I had that I knew he put value on, and I promised myself I would be generous with them when the time came.

Though it was still early in the morning, certainly by Greek standards, there were already a few customers in the store. The three women shoppers took curious and surreptitious glances at us, as did the pair of clerks waiting on them, but it was the store's owner himself, whom Win introduced as Mister Willford—"Everyone just calls him Tom, though"—who hurried to take care of us. No mere clerks for us, it seemed. The Rawleys might be poor, but it was quickly evident, in Mister Willford's toadying manner and the looks we got from the others, that here, at least, they were still regarded as a kind of aristocracy. I wondered what these people would think if they knew how poor we really were, and how hard the family worked to maintain a false façade. How hard, I corrected myself, Branston worked, since it did not seem to me that the others toiled greatly. Branston might be a bastard, but he was a hard working one, that was evident to me already. There was no question that it was his doing that people here still thought we were special.

But, away from home and Branson, Win had adopted a subtle air of superiority: cordial, but a trifle distant too. I realized with secret amusement that it was almost an imitation of Branston, but not so mean-spirited. I saw too that Mister Tom Willford did not mind at all, but even seemed to expect it.

"So this is the new relation?" Mister Willford said, measuring me with a clothier's experienced eye, already discerning sizes and cuts.

"New to these parts, anyway," Win said. "We need a suit to start, Tom. Nothing too fancy, mind, and none of those jacked up prices of yours either. Just a good quality suit for all occasions."

"Nothing fancy." Willford nodded his head in understanding, and led us to a rack filled with men's suits. The two of them began to look through the suits, debating, and paying little heed to me. Which I did not mind, since I had never bought or owned a suit in my life and would not have known what to look for in one.

I do not know what "fancy" constituted to their way of thinking, but I had certainly never owned anything as wonderful as the linen suit they settled on. I did not even mind that they never asked my opinion. It was just as well. If I had been asked to choose, I would have looked first for the least expensive one. I would never have dared ask for anything so special.

They picked some trousers for me too, Mister Willford suggesting different ones and Win eyeing them critically, and fingering the fabric, and a jacket. There were a half dozen shirts as well, and a pair of ties and new shoes so highly polished they hurt the eyes to look at them. We got everything, indeed, that Win deemed a necessary wardrobe for me to assume the role of a Rawley aristocrat. I noted with some amusement, however, that we did not buy me any underwear. That part of my wardrobe, at least, Win was apparently satisfied to leave as it was.

I tried everything on, and Mister Willford pinned cuffs up and checked sleeves and fitted the jackets. "I will have everything ready in an hour or so," he told Win when I had tried on the last of them.

"We'll go have us some lunch," Win said, "And come back in a bit."

We ate at the lunch counter in the bus depot. I had an American style hamburger dripping with grease and tasting delicious, and crisp, hot French fried potatoes on the side, and something to drink that Win called a chocolate malted, which was cold and sweet and which I immediately decided was, after a juicy male appendage, my very favorite food.

When we had finished, we went back to the store. The trousers had already been hemmed by then, and the jacket tailored to fit my broad shoulders and narrow waist. I tried them all on again, to be sure that Win was satisfied, and then Mister Willford sent his clerks to wrap everything up for us. Our arms filled with packages, we made our way back to the station wagon.

"There is a pioneer museum down the street," Win said, depositing everything on the back seat of the car. "If you like, we can spend a half hour or so there before we head back. It is moderately interesting. Or," he paused and gave me a smile, "We can stop on the way home and fuck, and tell everybody we visited the pioneer museum. I'll leave up to you to decide."

It was an easy choice, as I saw it. Anyway, I was determined that I would repay him for his generosity. "I expect I will have lots of chances in the future to see the pioneer museum," I said, smiling back.

* * * * * * *

We took the same road back as before, but about half way there, he turned off on a little side road, not much more than a lane, and after a mile or so along that he pulled to the side and parked by a thick stand of trees. There was an old blanket folded up in the back of the car and Win got that to take along and we climbed over a little fence, no more than a couple of boards. The grass here was tall and lush, and looked as if no one had come this way in some time. Only a few feet into the woods we came upon a clearing by a small, fast running stream. I looked around. It was a perfect trysting place, and I wondered how many times before he had come here. When I looked back the way we had come, I found that I could not see the car or the road through the greenery—which meant, if anybody should come by on the road, they would not see us, either. I quickly took my pecker out of my pants, eager to give him a real meal of it, but he shook his head and began to take his clothes off.

"Strip out of them things," he said, "And hang your clothes on one of the branches of the tree, there. We don't want to get home with any telltale grass stains on them. Best not to raise any suspicions."

I quickly did as he instructed. Naked, he spread the blanket on the ground and, with my own clothes hanging now in the tree with his, I joined him on it. I had always enjoyed being naked in the open sunlight. The sun was a good lover, in my experience, but Win quickly set to work doing his part. He gave my cock a kiss and a couple of quick tongue flicks, and then kissed and tongued my body all over.

I knew, of course, what he was angling for when he went to work with his tongue on my backside, but it felt just fine, and it was not going to get him what he wanted, so I relaxed and let him have the pleasure of it. He licked and fingered with determined ardor but when he tried to work a finger inside I pulled away from him and said, "Tongue it all you want but no fingers."

After a second try, with the same results, he gave up came back to my cock and sucked me while I looked happily up at a clear blue sky. A blackbird hovered overhead, seeming to take note of what we were doing, and with a disapproving cry, sailed away.

The sky was blotted out then when Win climbed up over me and put his stiff cock in my face. I lifted my head a little and took it in my mouth, one hand fondling his swaying balls, and gave him a generous sampling of my very best cocksucking; which, I may say, is pretty good indeed. It is easy to do something well when you truly love what you are doing.

Being in Kentucky was proving to be not so terrible after all, never mind what a son of a bitch Branston was. There were sunlit glades to take ones pleasure in as we were now. I could see that the townspeople looked up to me as part of their local aristocracy, which was something entirely new to me. I had a whole new wardrobe, which again was something I had never had before; and Win was available to keep my cock well exercised. Things could be a great deal worse, I thought, and ran my hand along the crack of his ass, till my finger found his little hole. I gave it a tentative poke.

"Are you saving yours for anyone special?" I asked, taking his cock out of my mouth."

"If I was," he said, turning over on his knees with his butt in the air, "You would surely be it. Just be gentle, though. I have not had it that way more than once or twice, and it has been a long time. You will find it tight, I am sure."

I hoped that was not intended to discourage me, since my dick stiffened even harder when he said it. I knelt behind him and took a minute or two to loosen him up with my fingers and lots of spit. He had told the truth, it was plenty tight, all right, but I got a finger worked well inside and I could tell from the way his cock was dancing about that he was enjoying having it up there, so I reckoned he was ready for bigger and better things.

I slicked up my knob with some more spit and pushed it against his little hole. It resisted at first, but my dick was on the trail now and it was not to be denied. I pushed harder and his hole yielded. He grunted once or twice, but he pushed back at me to help me. I worked it in slowly but steadily, and paused when I finally got the head well planted inside him.

"Jesus, that is enormous," he said in a strained voice.

I had always wanted sex to be mutual fun; my partner's pleasure always enhanced my own, and I hesitated briefly. "Should I stop," I asked, though my aching balls were telling me otherwise.

He gave a coarse laugh and wiggled his ass energetically for an answer. "You fucking crazy?" he asked. "I just said it was enormous, I didn't say I didn't love it."

Which was all the encouragement I needed. I began to shove again, taking my time—my pecker was plenty fat and where I was going was plenty slim—but I soon enough got the whole length of it in that hot little tunnel, clear up to my balls.

He had not lied about loving it, either, tight or not. When I commenced to ride him in earnest, pulling back and then shoving it home again, he began to moan with pleasure and grind his butt against my crotch with every thrust. Truth to tell, I do not think I had ever butt fucked anybody who loved it as much as he so obviously did, and I surely was not being gentle by this time. I reached around him and took hold of his erection and began to beat it furiously while I set to ramrodding him with a vengeance.

"Oh, shit, yes," he cried, gasping, "That's the way, boy, fuck me, fuck me hard, harder…ohh…ahh…."

His cock jerked in my hand and began to shoot, spilling over my pounding fist, and it set me off too. I fired a load like a cannon going off somewhere close to his ribcage, it felt like.

Softer now, my dick slipped out of him and I fell back on the blanket, my hands behind my head again. Grinning contentedly, he stretched out alongside me and used a corner of the blanket to wipe me clean.

"I don't know if you are the best thing that ever happened to us, or the worst," he said after a couple of minutes, fondling my dick lovingly. "Landing out of the blue amidst a frustrated bunch of letches like us. You could fuck all of us to death, I expect, and nobody would complain if you was to."

"Nobody but Branston," I said.

He sighed. "Yes, Branston surely would." He looked up at the sky. The sun was descending toward the horizon. "Speaking of which, Christ Almighty, it's late, we had better be getting our asses home. One of them is mighty sore, I can tell you true."

"Sorry if I was too rough," I said, splashing myself clean with some water from the creek.

He did the same, and we began to dress. "You were born to the saddle, boy," he said with a contented chuckle. "I never knew anybody could ride like that."

* * * * * * *

It was near dark by the time we reached home. There was barely time to clean up and to dress for dinner. Leticia came in while I was unwrapping my packages and held my new suit up to admire it.

"My, that is lovely," she said, "I can't wait to see it on you.

"It was so kind of Win to buy all this for me," I said, "I surely hope he does not get into any trouble with Branston over it, spending all that money the way he did."

"Win?" She gave me a surprised look. "That wasn't his money he was spending. This was entirely Branston's doing. He told Win to take you into town and see that you got everything you needed."

* * * * * * *

I am sure I never in my whole life took more care with dressing than I did on this occasion. I wore the new suit and I tied and retied the necktie before I was satisfied that it was perfect and although the new shoes were already as shiny as satin, I spit on them and rubbed them to give them even more of a sheen. I got my hair to behave, too, or mostly, though by the time I got downstairs to the library a pair of devilish curls had already fallen over one eye.

I went straight to where Branston sat in his chair reading a newspaper, and stood before him at attention until he lowered the paper and looked up at me.

"Thank you, sir," I said in my politest voice. "For the clothes."

He looked me up and down and fingered the fabric of my coat, and even glanced down at those shoes, so that I was glad I had given them the extra shine. His expression re-mained unchanged, but he said, "You look nice."

My face broke into an ear-to-ear grin and if I had not thought he would boot me for it, I would have flung myself upon him and kissed those luscious lips. I had to restrain my-self with a real effort.

"After this, though," he said, "Wear the jacket and trousers to dinner, and save the suit for good. You have got time for a drink, boy, if you have a mind for one."

I looked happily in Win's direction. "A glass of wine, I think," I said, since I could see that was what Leticia and Ellen were sipping.

Branston had gone back to his newspaper, but he said, not looking up, "Rawley men drink bourbon. Kentucky bourbon. You can have it with branch water, if you think it's too potent plain."

I blushed and was all mad at him again. Really, the man was impossible to get along with, no matter how hard you tried.

"I will have it plain," I told Win, loud enough to be sure the man in the chair heard me. I would not have him think I was some kind of sissy.

Win poured me a glass of the amber liquid and handed it to me with a little congratulatory nod and a quick wink. I was about to take a sip when Branston asked, "What was that name again? Speye-row?"

I was glad he had his nose buried in his newspaper, since I was still angry with him, and I did not want him to see my little grin.

"Spee-row," I said, enunciating it precisely.

I almost choked on my first taste of Kentucky bour-bon.

◙ CHAPTER FOUR ◙
▲

Dinner was more pork, chops this time, which made me think of those hogs in the pen behind the barn. Well, they surely were not there as pets. There were more greens, too, and more boiled potatoes. It was plain food, as I had been warned, but it was hearty, and plentiful. I ate better on this occasion, and took a peculiar pleasure in the fact that he noticed.

"It's good for a man to eat hearty," he said, "It means he is healthy and sober. It's the sick and silly ones don't eat right."

I immediately piled some more food on my plate and shoveled it heartily into my mouth, but with that bit of wisdom he turned his attention back to his own food and ignored me again.

Since Win's daughter, Ellen, was no more than a few years older than me, I had thought her a likely candidate for friendship, but she showed no interest in it. She was surly and withdrawn as she had been before, and answered my few attempts at conversation with no more than "yes," and "no."

I shrugged that off. I had already noted that conversation at the table was desultory, at best. Leticia asked Win a question or two about people in town, but that subject was quickly exhausted, since except for our visit to the store and the lunch counter at the depot, most of our time had been spent fucking in the woods; though, of course, he was not likely to tell her about that. He did mention that we had stopped at the pioneer museum for a spell. Luckily, no one asked me any questions about it. I had forgotten to think up any answers in advance. Really, I would have to make an actual visit to that museum at the first opportunity, just to be safe.

I did take a perverse bit of pleasure in noting that Win sat rather gingerly in his chair throughout dinner and with every indication that his bottom was still sore from the plowing I had given it. For all the enthusiasm he had shown for my company while we had been at it, however, Win was utterly aloof with me when we were together in Branston's presence and in fact treated me in a distant manner, as if he hadn't the slightest interest in me.

The few times Branston spoke directly to him, Win looked terrified, but I saw whenever he looked at Branston without Branston's awareness, Win looked at him with utter loathing.

I saw, too, though, what I had guessed before and what I suspect Win himself was not altogether aware of: his desire for the man he loathed. Win was no more impervious to Branston's nearly overwhelming aura of masculine sensuality than I was. Branston was like some fine breeding stud, you could not look at him without thinking of sex in every possible variety—and in my case, I imagined one or two I was sure probably were not possible, but entertaining to contemplate nevertheless. I was certain of one thing: no one short of a dead person would be able to refuse him if he asked. For that matter, I sort of doubted that he deigned very often to ask. I thought he was probably a man to give it where he chose, and had no doubts that the recipient would be glad for the gift. I know that I would have been.

Which caused me to wonder about something. Who was this god-among-mortals giving it to, here on this isolated farm? I had seen or heard nothing to indicate that he went away anywhere to take his pleasures. Mrs. Corey seemed an unlikely outlet, and it appeared we had no hired hands. That left Leticia and Ellen and Win, who clearly were not getting any; and me, and, regretfully, neither was I.

I stole a glance across the table at Ellen. She was pretty enough, I guess; but the two of them obviously despised one another, so that was an unlikely possibility, as I saw it.

Of course, he could just be jerking off regularly, I supposed, but I could not imagine that would long remain satisfactory to anyone so highly charged as Branston seemed to be. Still, I did not see any other possibilities. It was possible, of course, that he had a mistress stashed away somewhere here on the farm that I did not know of. I made a mental note to poke around at those various outbuildings when I had the opportunity, but I do not think I had much expectation of learning anything.

Well, what of it, I thought? They were all isolated here, and all highly charged up, it seemed to me. Win seemed to have been doing without before I got here, and he was plenty hot blooded; and Leticia was so cock-crazy that, if Win were to be believed, she had made a practice of just about raping any man who came within range. She had certainly tried with me. As for Ellen, I knew nothing about her sex habits, but she had the same fiery look in her eyes as the rest of them. How in the name of heaven had they stood it for any length of time, I wondered, penned up here with one another the way they were?

Branston had finished eating while I puzzled over this. I had already fathomed that no one left the table before him. He stood now and excused himself to Leticia and started from the room, but to my surprise he paused by my chair, startling me so badly that I dropped my fork with a bang on my plate. I grabbed it up hastily and managed to look wide-eyed up at him.

"The women like to watch television after dinner," he said. "And Win, of course. Myself, I finish up the outside chores and then I see to the paperwork in my office. I'm not much of a one for idling. I sent you to bed early last night because I figured you were tired from your journey, but you are free to do as you wish with your evenings."

It seemed to me that he was offering me a challenge. I could waste my time with the women—and Win—or I could...or I could what? I was tempted to suggest that I join him, but he had not invited me to do that and I did not want to risk yet another rebuff by pushing myself forward. The silence in the room seemed weighty while I considered.

"I saw that there are plenty of books in the library," I said, "And I can use the practice with my English. If it is all right with you, sir, I think I will read."

I could not tell from that expressionless face whether my answer had pleased him or not. All he said was, "There is no shortage of books there. Help yourself to them," and he started again for the door, but once more he paused.

"I will remind you that morning comes early. This is a working farm," he said, and then he truly was gone. It seemed to me like much of the energy left the room with him.

Win said to me, "I'll watch television with the women. I'm not much of a one for reading."

"You come join us if you get bored," Leticia said.

Ellen said nothing.

* * * * * * *

There was indeed no shortage of books to choose from, as Branston had said, but many of those in the library were probably beyond my limited ability at reading English. I was not ready for college textbooks, and the few novels did not much interest me, nor did a section of cookbooks, though I thought it odd that they were in here and not in the kitchen, where they might have served some purpose. I thumbed through a couple of these just out of curiosity. The pictures were pretty, at any event.

I took a large and well-thumbed volume down from the shelf and glanced at its cover. Farming Methods and Practices sounded a bit dry, but when I considered it, I thought it might be worth my while to spend some time with it. I had come to live on a farm, had I not? And I was going to be expected to earn my keep. I took the book with me and settled into a chair but changed my mind almost at once. I got up and went instead to Branston's chair and snuggled up in it. I felt sure that this was as close as I would ever get to that sculpted ass of his.

56

The book was dry reading, and some of it taxed my limited English, but I read determinedly on—about tobacco and burley and limestone soil. I learned about livestock, spending a few minutes extra on hog breeding; and thoroughbred horses, which made me think of the big dick Branson showed in his trousers. I moved on to cattle, which was certainly safer to contemplate.

I fell asleep in the dairy products.

* * * * * * *

I was back in Greece, a little boy again, and my father was shaking me gently awake. His big hand was tender and loving, and I turned and kissed the back of it, savoring the wiry hair that grew there and the manly scent of him.

Only, it came to me gradually, something was different. The scent was not my father's scent of Greek olives and fish from the Aegean; it was the scent of tobacco. And manure.

I opened my eyes suddenly, jerking my lips away from the hand touching me, and looked up into a pair of amethyst pools. Branston stood over me, regarding me in that solemn way he had. I sat bolt upright, my mouth hanging open, but I could find nothing to say.

"Seems like you had best take yourself off to bed, boy" Branston said. He made no comment on the fact that I was in his chair; and certainly none about that kiss I had given his hand, though he had removed that discretely from my shoulder.

"Yes, sir," I said, and jumped to my feet, letting the book fall from my lap to the floor with a loud thump.

He rescued it before I could, and glanced at its title before handing it back to me. "Might as well take it with you," he said. "If you have any difficulty sleeping, this should surely do the trick."

I snatched the book from his hand, and fled for my room.

* * * * * * *

I dreamed of him, dreamed that he was on the bed, straddling me. He kissed me with those ripe, full lips of his, and moved downward, his tongue igniting flames across my throat, my chest, my belly. His mouth found my ready cock and he took it, and began to suck and lick it hungrily.

Only, I realized belatedly that I was not dreaming any longer. Someone really was sucking my cock, very well and very enthusiastically. Win, I supposed, come for a midnight snack. Well, I did not mind, my dream of Branston had gotten my blood boiling and I was not more than a second or two from shooting a load.

I put my hand down, and ran my fingers through the fine, soft hair. Too much of it, I realized suddenly, but it was too late to hold myself back. My cock exploded in an eruption of come, one shot, two, three, squirting into the eagerly sucking mouth.

I finished, sinking breathlessly back against my pillow. The bed creaked and a minute later, the door opened. I had a mere glimpse of Leticia in the pale light from the hallway before it closed again.

I groaned and rolled over, shoving my damp cock against the bed sheet, and fell asleep at once.

* * * * * * *

I woke to Ellen's tap at the door. For a moment I could not think why the sheet beneath me should be sticky with come residue. Then I blushed, remembering that nocturnal visit from Leticia. She had not had to rape me, not exactly, at least; but still, I liked to choose who got my cream. I made a mental note to lock my door at night after this.

I forgot about her quickly, though, when I remembered waking up earlier in the library and finding Branston bending over me while I slept. He had not seemed to be angry, even about my kissing his hand in my sleep; but it was hard to read his moods. Now, if it had only been he during the night…just thinking about him made my pulse quicken.

I jumped out of bed and dressed in a hurry, in my old jeans and a tee shirt and my battered sneakers, thinking about him the whole time. I looked at myself in the mirror over the dresser, and my homely face looked ridiculously eager even to my own eyes. I thought for a moment and changed the plain white tee shirt for a bright red one that made my skin look tawny and my green eyes like emeralds. Not that he was likely to notice, but I wanted to look as good as I could for him anyway.

I was not sure how I should deal with Leticia this morning, but when I saw her at the breakfast table she acted as if nothing at all had happened. If she was embarrassed in any way, she concealed it perfectly. I almost thought maybe it had only been a wet dream after all, but I knew it had not been.

Win seemed moody, which made me wonder if he knew about her little visit to my bedroom. Ellen was distant, as she usually was, and Branston was his uncommunicative self, though I looked up once and saw that he was watching me as if wondering about something. I suppose it was because I was eating ravenously. Whether it was the excitement of shopping yesterday, or the sex, or the sexy thoughts I could not stop entertaining about him, something had given me a hearty appetite.

When he had finished his breakfast, Branston rose from the table, but he spoke directly to me before he went out.

"This is a farm, as you know," he said, "And we have to work hard to make it produce. Everyone has to work. You will have to as well."

"I am not afraid of work, sir," I said. "If you will just tell me what I should do."

He nodded—approvingly, I thought—and considered that for a minute. "Win takes care of things around the house, when he is not idling around town picking up travelers and shopping. Probably the women can use some help, if that is more to your liking."

I had an idea that maybe he was giving me another of his challenges. I was beginning to understand he liked testing people, giving them the opportunity to reveal what they were made of.

"I like to work outside, sir, and I am strong. I can do man's work," I said. "I will come to work with you, if that is all right."

He nodded. "Fine. But I'm clearing some land today. That's a real job. Come if you like, but I don't tolerate any whining."

"I do not whine," I said, sticking my chin up, "And I am not afraid of hard work."

He left without replying and I sat for a moment wondering if I was supposed to just follow him. But, on consideration, I realized he was not likely to come back and give me a special invitation. I gave the others a nod, ignoring Win's somewhat sardonic smile, and went quickly after Branston. It was not that I was particularly looking forward to what sounded like hard physical labor, but there was one consolation in it: I would be with him all day.

I caught up with him outside the barn. He was already loading tools into the back of that battered pickup truck. He glanced at me briefly, and continued what he was doing. And since he had not given me any instructions, I stood quietly by and waited for him to finish.

When he was done loading the truck he swung himself up into the driver's seat. "Hop in, if you're coming," he said, and the truck was already moving by the time I had jumped in the other side.

The truck was as uncomfortable as it looked. Whatever springs had once softened its ride had long since given up trying, and my bottom soon felt like it had been given a good spanking, from bouncing up and down on the hard seat.

He drove slowly, of necessity, the truck lumbering and swaying over an unplanted field, but even driving slowly he managed to make that ungainly truck seem just another attachment to his body. We drove in silence for a long time, but for a change, it was a companionable silence. I decided I had made the right decision, to come work with him. I had an idea that maybe he was pleased. Or as pleased, it seemed, as he ever got about anything.

Out of the blue, he asked me, "Has anyone been pestering you since you got here?"

At first I did not grasp what he meant. When I did, I blushed and looked away, out the window, to hide my embarrassment.

"No," I lied. I did not think he would be happy to hear the truth.

He did not say anything again for another long while, and I was afraid to look at him. Finally, he said, "I guess you are old enough to make up your own mind about things."

We grew silent again. I took his remark to mean that he knew about Leticia, and Win, and their sexual inclinations. Of course, I did not suppose Branston missed much that went on there. That being so, I wondered how much he might or might not know, or guess, about me. Most American men, as I understood it, disapproved of man love. Maybe, I thought, that was why he acted hard toward me.

I dismissed that thought, though, as quickly as it had come. He was no different toward the others than he was toward me. Maybe he was even harder on them. I wondered if he had always been like this, and I tried briefly to imagine him acting silly, laughing, cutting up the way most young men did—he was, after all, still a young man, I don't think he could have been more than thirty, if that—but the images would not come. I suspected he was born glowering at people, with his eyes sparking angrily.

For as poor as we were supposed to be, the Rawley fields seemed to me to go on forever. Most of them were planted in what I recognized as tobacco. Americans must smoke a lot, was all I could think. Luckily, I suppose, for us. Though Branston himself did not appear to do so. Since I did not, myself, I rather liked that about him. Men who smoked, like Win, had the smell about them that never did seem to get washed off. Branston smelled of man smells, sweat and clean skin and the aroma, so faint that I probably only wishfully imagined it, of his sex.

We finally left the rows of tobacco behind and bounced our way up and down some small hills, ducking trees as we went, maple and birch and elm, and others I did not recognize. Finally he slowed further and stopped the truck in a clearing. There had been trees growing thickly here too, not long ago, but most of them were stumps, now, and here and there were holes in the ground where stumps had already been removed.

"This is what you meant by clearing some land," I said, getting out my side. "I was not sure. Sometimes my English is a little confused."

He might have made one of his cutting remarks about that, but he did not. He seemed to be in a particularly mellow mood; maybe it was because I had volunteered to work with him. He began to unload the tools from the back of the truck.

"We need it for planting," he said. "If I am ever going to get this place on its feet, I need to increase the harvest. That takes more land."

"But, you mean, you have been doing it all by yourself?" Even I could see, looking around, that it was a tremendous amount of work. It was hard to imagine that one man, even one as big and strong as Branston obviously was, could have done it without help.

He actually half-grinned at that. "Can you see Win out here swinging an axe?" he asked. "Even Leticia would be more likely than him. We don't have any hands, except rare times when there is extra work. Harvest, say, when it has to be done fast while the weather holds. Then we have got no choice but to hire some hands. But this, well, I have been doing it myself, yes."

"But there are so many trees, and they are so big," I said, still astonished, but apparently that discussion was over.

"We can't afford hired hands," he said with finality. "You are living here now, and you are part of the family, so you might as well know how things stand. They had hands before, and they were also spending twice as much every month as they were bringing in. No place can go on like that for long. We are ten years in debt already, without hiring folks to do our work for us. I will do it myself."

"Well, I will help," I told him, "It does not look like it could be too hard to learn."

"No, it is not hard to learn," he agreed, with what I thought was an amused expression. He took an axe for himself and handed me another. He made it seem like his was light as a feather, but when I went to take mine from him, the weight so surprised me that I let it fall out of my hand and nearly chopped off my own foot. I picked it up again. Fortunately, he did not seem to have noticed.

"Take that one," he said, pointing at what even I could see was one of the puniest trees in the woods, a young oak that had hardly begun to get its growth.

I was about to tell him that I could do better than that, but I bit my tongue. I would show him with deeds rather than words. I would quickly make toothpicks out of his damn little sprout of a tree, and then he would see that I meant business about working.

"Great," I said, altogether indifferent. I pretended that I did not see him take a swing with his axe at the biggest damn tree of all. He buried the blade in it with one mighty swing, and paused.

"Hot," he said, looking my way and taking off his shirt, "And it gets hotter when you work."

I took that to be a suggestion, and I followed his example, taking my time because it gave me the opportunity to take a good long look at him without his shirt. The muscles in his arms and chest rippled seductively in the golden sunlight as he began to chop at his tree again.

"You gorgeous bastard," I thought. I sighed and took a hard swing at my own tree—and immediately I discovered a flaw in my plan to show him I meant business. That puny looking oak tree was apparently made of rock, or else my axe blade was dull. The blade had barely penetrated the tree trunk.

I ran a finger surreptitiously along the edge of the blade. It seemed plenty sharp enough. I took another look at the tree. It appeared to be of ordinary wood, like any other tree. I let fly again, putting everything I had into the swing. The blade sank in this time, but only just. It dawned on me then that I was in for one hell of a morning.

In a matter of minutes my arms and shoulders were aching and a river of sweat ran down my chest. Worse, I had barely made a start of bringing down the tree. I stole a glance in Branston's direction. He swung his axe as if it weighed nothing, wood chips flying with each blow. His tree was enormous compared to mine, and the way we were going, he would have his down before I got halfway through mine. Determined, I started up again.

The sun got hotter. I was not weak and I was not lazy, but I had never done this kind of physical labor before. I had begun to ache in places I had never known I had muscles. Worse, I did not even have to look at the sky to know it was not yet more than mid-morning. The day had barely started.

I could not help it; I had to stop after a little while. I rested the axe on the ground and wiped a hand across my sweaty brow, breathing hard.

"If you can't handle it," Branston called without pausing, "You can head back to the house. There's plenty back there you can busy yourself with. I doubt the eggs have been collected from the henhouse yet."

I was going to be assigned to collecting eggs? Like some old woman? That set fire to my Mediterranean temper. "I am not even winded," I called back. I managed to somehow pick up the axe again and start swinging with it, but I was in a daze by now and my numb arms seemed to move of their own accord.

The sun got hotter and my sweat ran faster. I did not know if the buzzing I heard was in my head or the insects in the grass. All I could think of was what a rotten son of a bitch Branston Rawley was, and how I would prefer to use my axe on him rather than the stupid tree. I would happily chop him into pieces and feed them to the crows. Of course, I would save his dick to mount on the wall as a trophy.

I did not know he had stopped chopping until I saw him standing the other side of my tree, though he was surely in no danger from my faltering blade. I lowered the axe, trying not to show how grateful I was for the pause, and pushed a wet stray curl off my forehead.

"What is wrong?" I asked, trying without much success not to sound winded.

"Nothing wrong," he said. "It's time we took a break, is all."

"I am just fine, thank you," I managed to say, but when I tried to pick up the axe again, it would not come.

64

He stepped around the tree and put a hand on my shoulder. "There's a thermos of iced tea in the truck. Why don't you bring it up to that patch of shade on the hill there? I could surely use some."

He started up the hill with that rolling gait of his. I was glad he had insisted. I leaned the axe handle against the tree gratefully and went to get the iced tea from the front seat of the truck.

The drive here to the field had brought us uphill gradually, so I did not actually realize how high we were till I joined him where he sat in the grass leaning against the trunk of a big maple tree, its leafy branches providing a welcome shade from the sun and rustling faintly in the breeze. A wide panorama lay spread out at our feet, the gentle green hills rolling down to a wide valley, and the Cumberland River winding its way through the sea of green. The distant hills beyond the river looked gray and purple from here.

I sat beside him in the cool shade and poured a cup of the icy tea. There was just the one cup and I handed it to him first. He half-emptied the cup and handed it back to me. I tried inconspicuously to put my lips on the exact same spot his had touched, and emptied the cup. The tea was utterly welcome, cold and sweet; or maybe, I thought, that was the lingering taste of his lips that made it so sweet. I was no longer angry with him.

"It is beautiful here," I said, filling the cup again and handing it to him once again. From the corner of my eye I saw that he too drank from the same spot as before, though in his case it was merely by chance. He seemed almost surprised by my remark, looking at me and then out over the valley of the Cumberland.

"Yes, it is that," he agreed. We were silent for a while before he said, "I was away from here for many years. I suppose Win told you all about that."

"Not all," I said. "He said you had been away, but he did not say where." Or why, I thought, but I left that unsaid.

"I was lots of different places," he said. "I saw just about all this country, I reckon, and parts of some others." He was still staring at the view, so I could look at him while he talked. He was different all of a sudden, not so hard and cold as he usually was. Something warm and gentle had softened his voice and his expression. And he was still the handsomest man I had ever seen. I ate him up with my eyes, and longed to fling myself upon him.

"There's plenty of beautiful places in the world," he said. "Bigger hills, and mountains. Wider river, and trees...did you ever hear tell of the redwoods out in California? They are as big as a house, just about the biggest things that grow in the world, they say."

"I can not imagine trees that big," I said. Greece was a land of few trees, only the twisted olives that provided much of the natives' sustenance.

"They are something to see, those redwoods" he said, and paused as if recalling them. "But for all the wonders that I saw," he went on, "I never stopped remembering this place. Kentucky, I mean. There's no place like it. Someday, I will take you around to see it all."

I could not help saying, with what was probably too much enthusiasm, "I would like that," but he seemed not to have heard.

"There's mountains clear over to the east," he said, "Not those massive things they have in California or Colorado, but green and beautiful and rounded, like a woman's breasts. And horses, Kentucky has the most beautiful horses in the world, and the blue grass up around Lexington, that's something to see, it's like looking at the waves of an ocean when it blows in the breeze. And rivers, why, there's a paddlewheel steamer still goes up and down the Ohio, you will have to ride that someday. And we got woods here just like what they were when the Indians lived in them. All this sky, and the clean air, and room for a man to move around in."

It was the most I had ever heard him say, and I realized suddenly what was different about him: he was a man in love. In love with the beautiful view at our feet, in love with the rolling hills and the trees and the green fields. It was a strange kind of thrill for me to share the moment with him. In another way, though, it was embarrassing too, as if I were witness to something private, something not meant to be shared.

The moment of intimacy went as suddenly as it had come. He gave me a sideways look, as if he were surprised to find me there, and stood up abruptly. "We've wasted enough time, I reckon," he said shortly. "There's trees to be felled."

Having rested, I was able to pick up my axe again and start back to work, and by lunchtime I had actually managed to get my tree down and was ready to start another one; at least in theory, but in truth, I had gotten very stiff, and not in places where I usually enjoyed it.

We had sandwiches, big slabs of cold salty ham on fresh baked bread, and crisp apples that crunched when you bit into them and sent sweet juices running down your chin. He was not so talkative this time, but his silence was not unfriendly like it had been before, and it seemed to me that there had been a big change in our relationship. Even with the soreness in my muscles, it felt wonderful to be sitting in the grass alongside him, stealing glances at him whenever I could without being conspicuous. He went a short distance away to pee noisily, but I was too scared to try to peek at him then, lest he catch me at it and be angry. I took my own turn a bit nearer, but of course, he had no interest in looking at me.

Given my choice, I would have sat there all day with him, in the shade of the maple tree, but we had to go back to work eventually. At least he put our axes back into the bed of the truck, and instead we used a saw, each taking an end, and set to work on one of the biggest trees. It was hard work too, but nowhere near as hard as the chopping. I had a notion that he was showing consideration for my weariness, and I could not help but be grateful.

I do not remember ever feeling as tired as I was by the time we finally packed it in and climbed into the truck, and got back to the house late that day. What I wanted more than anything was to crawl into my bed and pass out from fatigue; but I knew that he would see that as evidence of my weakness and I was determined that was not going to happen. I took a long shower, letting the water wash away some of the stiffness, and dressed, in the correct jacket and trousers this time, and at seven thirty on the dot, I came down to the library.

"How was your day of man's work?" Win asked first thing, looking somehow amused.

"Great," I said enthusiastically. "I could really learn to love this life." I looked Branston's way in time to catch his quick glance over the top of his newspaper, but I could not see his expression. "I believe I will have some bourbon," I told Win.

The bourbon sent some welcome fire through me and helped me get through the evening. Dinner came and went. I was so tired I could hardly keep my eyes open, but I managed to eat nevertheless—eat quite heartily, as a matter of fact.

"My goodness," Leticia said at one point, "You have got an appetite tonight, haven't you?"

"Let him be. He's earned it," Branston said, without looking at me.

I did not feel half as weary after that. I even, when I got up to my room, remembered to lock the door and managed to get one shoe off before I fell across the bed and into a deep, dreamless sleep.

◎ CHAPTER FIVE ◎

▲

If I thought I had suffered the day before, though, it was nothing compared to the agony I felt when I woke the next morning. I tried to sit up in bed and found I could barely move. Every muscle in my body had turned to stone; painful, aching stone.

It took forever to get myself showered and dressed, and I barely made it down in time for breakfast. Branston glanced at me as I hurried in, but as usual it was impossible to tell what he was thinking.

"Are you ailing?" Leticia asked, looking concerned at me when I sat down gingerly in my chair.

"I am fine," I assured her, and refused to look at Branston, though he seemed to take no notice of my awkward movements. But then, he generally took little notice of me, so that probably meant nothing.

After breakfast, we again loaded up the truck and drove to the backfields where we had worked the day before. Branston did, however, acknowledge that he had some inkling of what kind of shape I was in.

"I imagine you are a little stiff and sore today," he said, which was certainly an understatement. "It will be worse for you, though, if you don't loosen those muscles up today. Take it slow to start, and you'll be okay by lunchtime."

I was grateful for his concern, and I took his suggestion, working slowly, not trying to prove myself the way I had the day before. He was right: my muscles did begin to loosen up after a bit. They were still sore when we broke for lunch, but nowhere near as sore as they had been when I started, and I came home from my days work considerably less exhausted than I had the previous day.

I ate greedily again, and I actually thought I saw Branston look at me approvingly once, though I might have been mistaken.

* * * * * * *

I woke early in the morning, before Ellen's tap on the door, even. For the first time since I had arrived, I was happy to have a new day beginning. A day I would be spending with Branston.

It was barely dawn. The house had not yet begun to stir. I slipped out of the bed went to the French doors and stepped naked on to my little balcony. Not that I was interested in showing off my nudity, but even if anyone did look, they would see me only from the waist up.

Below, Branston walked across the lawn in the direction of the barns, a pail in each hand. It occurred to me that he was up every day long before everyone else, already at work hours before I joined him in the fields; and in the evenings too, when I was washing away the sweat of my day's toil and bemoaning my aching muscles, he was finishing up the chores, which often he barely finished by dinnertime, and later, he worked in his office—sometimes, it seemed half the night.

On an impulse, I dressed quickly and hurried down the stairs and out of the house. I found him in the barn, just finishing milking the half dozen cows, the milk squirting noisily into the buckets. He looked up, surprised, when I joined him, and the cows, too, gave me curious looks over their shoulders, as if uncomfortable being interrupted at their toilette.

"You're up mighty early," Branston said, puzzled.

"No earlier than you are," I said. "I have come to help with the farm work."

"Seems to me like you're putting in a good day's work as it is," he said. "Out in the field. I can see you are working hard."

"I am not a baby," I said. "If you can work sun up to sundown, there is no reason I should be sitting on my behind doing nothing." I looked around. "What else is there to do?"

It was impossible of course to tell from his expressionless face if he was pleased or not. "Those stalls needs sweeping out," he said, indicating the holding pens along one wall. "If you have got your heart set on working. And the hogs need feeding. And the horse."

I saw to the livestock. There were the cows, of course, and three good-sized pigs and some piglets in a pen of their own behind the barn. The grown ones, he made me to understand, would be butchered in the fall, to provide those pork roasts we had been having for dinner and hams and bacon and all sorts of sausages, for the winter. The little ones would be the following year's eating. The babies were cute, and I stood atop the fence and reached down to pet one of them, and Branston, just behind me, called out sharply, "Careful, keep your hands out of there."

I jumped and almost fell into the pen, but he grabbed hold of my arm to steady me. I was conscious of his big, strong hand holding me, and sorry when it went away.

"A sow can be pretty vicious if she thinks anyone is messing with her little ones,' he said. "That one there, that's the mother, she weighs about three hundred pounds. If she ever knocked you down, you'd have a hell of a time getting back up. Never climb into the pen with them without someone to distract her."

I gave the pigs a wider berth after that, just standing outside their pen and tossing their food—some grain, and slops from the house—over the fence to them. They were noisy eaters, but I noticed that the mother sow kept a wary eye on me, like she thought I might have too much interest in her piglets. They were cute, all right, but my interest had been discouraged.

There were chickens to be fed also, and a single horse, a big bay that stood alone in his stall. He was still a handsome animal, but I could see that he was along in years. There was gray about his muzzle, and he looked at me with big, world-weary eyes. Something about him teased at my memory.

After a moment, I realized what it was—unless I was mistaken, this was the same horse in the portrait with Branston, the one that hung on the main staircase. This one had a distinctive mark on his forehead, very nearly a star, and I was sure I remembered that from the painting, too.

I wondered that Branston kept him on, since the horse did not appear likely to be of any use for work, and I had seen no one ride him; but I kept my questions to myself, not wanting Branston to think over much about feeding unnecessary guests.

* * * * * * *

After that, I helped him mornings and evenings, until he retired to his paperwork in his office, which I could certainly not help him with, though I would have been happy to keep him the company. I took special care with the old horse—it was the one from the painting, I was sure of that now. That star on his forehead was too unique to be mere coincidence.

I found myself standing, staring at the painting, at the horse and, of course, the boy standing alongside him. The arrogance that I had noticed when I first saw it was still there, but I thought now that I detected something else beneath it, all but hidden by the pose he so carefully assumed. I was not altogether sure of what it was, but there was something gentle there, too, and something that seemed to beseech the viewer, to ask for—but to ask for what?

Of course, I told myself, the artist could have added that from his own imagination. I found myself studying Branston covertly, looking for that same quality in the man that boy had become. At times, I thought I had found it; but at others, I was equally convinced I had only dreamed it. It

72

was hard to imagine that Branston ever had or ever would ask anyone for anything.

Certainly he had not asked me to put in the extra work, and I cannot say I was not tired by the time our day was done; indeed, for the next few days I walked around much of the time in a stupor of exhaustion. But it did seem to me as if he appreciated my help, and maybe even my company, such as it was, and I did take pleasure in having the entire day with him. I regretted only that I could not share the nighttime with him as well. I liked to think there were things I could help him with even then, but I felt sure he would not welcome my assistance in that direction.

I got stronger, too, as the days passed, and after a week, I found I could swing an axe all day long without suffering the pain of the damned for it afterward, and still have plenty of energy left over to feed chickens and pigs. It seemed as if I could all but see the muscles in my arms growing with every day, and my chest filled out to where my old tee shirt now fit me skin tight and would soon not go on at all. My skin was darker, too, from all the time in the sun, and I fairly glowed with health. I was not any handsomer than I had been before, but when I looked at myself in the mirror, turning this way and that and flexing my newly developed muscles, I felt that it was a man who looked back at me now, and not a boy.

Of course, I was still "boy" to Branston, but it no longer seemed condescending to me when he called me that. Working together as we were, our relationship inevitably and subtly began to change. I would not exactly say he treated me like a friend, not the way you usually use that term, but he was not unfriendly either, as he had been at first. I think he was coming to accept me, and I considered that even more of an accomplishment than the building of my muscles. I took pride in feeling that at least I was earning my keep now and could no longer be regarded as just a burden.

Branston even sometimes talked to me; real conversation, I mean, though it was mostly brief. He was not what you would call a talkative sort, and he certainly did not engage in idle chatter, and I took my cue from him and mostly spoke when spoken to.

One day, in the pickup truck on the way to the back-field, he surprised me by saying, out of the blue, "You think I'm mean to the rest of them, don't you?"

I was tempted to deny it, but instinct told me that I was once again being tested, and I thought that the truth, even the brutal truth, would be a better policy. "I think you are hard on them, yes, sir" I said.

I waited on tenterhooks while he concentrated on his driving and seemed to consider my reply. "I admire your honesty, boy," he said finally; and, after another pause, he said, "Do you think the poor house would be any easier for them? Because that's where they were headed, sure as shoot-ing."

"I never thought of it that way," I said.

"Anyway, you're no fool. Look at them. They can't any of them think past their crotches. They're monsters, the Rawleys, the whole bunch of them." He thought about that for a moment. "I guess I'm a monster, too, but at least I'm not a slave to my pecker. You know that word?"

"Yes," I said, praying he would not ask how I had learned it. It was not something you would find in an English grammar book in school.

If he wondered, though, he did not ask.

* * * * * * *

Now that I was over the initial shock of it, I found that life in Kentucky was not half bad, or so it seemed to me. Except that I had no social life. In Athens, there had been lovers and friends and lots of things to do at all times. Our routine here on the farm remained strict indeed. I was up early, ate breakfast put in a hard day's work. Then it was a glass of bourbon and dinner, and an hour or so before bed, which I usually spent reading. I was becoming a pretty fair farmer, at any rate, at least in terms of book knowledge.

I was not really alone, of course, but I could not help feeling isolated from the others. Win appeared to be jealous of my time with Branston, and had turned cool toward me. I had taken to locking my bedroom door at night to prevent any more nighttime visits from Leticia. Once I woke at night to the sound of the door being tried stealthily. I waited, in case it was Win. I thought if it was he would most likely call my name or knock. I would not have minded if it was him, since I was beginning to notice the lack of sexual activity

No one spoke, however, or knocked, and I thought I heard muted footsteps going softly away, so I decided that it was probably Leticia after all. After that, I heard no one try the door again, though most nights now I slept like a rock after my day's work. Leticia remained polite to me but she was not exactly chummy either. I spent all day with Branston, it was true, but though we were no longer at odds, we were not exactly buddies either.

Which left Ellen, and we were close enough in ages that I might have thought we would become friends, but we did not. I tried once or twice to make overtures in that direction but she kept me at arms length. She seemed particularly unhappy with her life here on the farm, and Win did unbend enough to tell me one evening something of her story.

"It's on account of her mother, my wife," he said, sitting by me on the porch steps. "I married the wrong woman, you see. The wrong woman, at least, in Branston's opinion. She was beneath our social level, as Branston saw it."

"But you were in love with her," I said. "How could he blame you for marrying the woman you loved?"

"I can't say that I did, particularly. Love her, I mean," he surprised me by saying. "I suppose I married her as much out of spite as anything, just to show my independence. The only time I ever did, I guess, now that I think of it."

"What happened to her, then?" I asked, thinking I was never going to understand these people.

"Oh, she put up with things for a while. In time, though, she ran off with another man, some traveling salesman. It all happened on the spur of the moment, I expect."

"Didn't she love you either?"

He shrugged. "Maybe she did, at first, anyway. That didn't stop her from going, though. I expect it was because she had been treated so coldly while she was here. It wasn't just Branston, either. Leticia wasn't any better. And if I was to be honest, I wasn't much of a husband to her. Didn't take any time to get her knocked up, you understand, I did manage to do that much, and I knew that Branston was unhappy to think of her child being a Rawley, so I was pleased enough to have accomplished that, and after that, why, I just plain lost interest in her, seemed like."

"And she never came back?" I asked.

He chuckled, but mirthlessly. "Oh, she came back, all right," he said, "But she was sick with the pox. Do you know what that is?"

I nodded, although in truth I had only the vaguest idea. Something, I was sure, that had to do with illicit sex, since almost everything connected with the Rawleys seemed to lead back to that one subject.

"Branston said she must have had it before she left, as it didn't happen that quick, but that I wouldn't know about. I didn't have it, I went to see the doctor and had some tests, to be sure of that, so if she got it while she was here, she got it from somewhere else, but I can't say. She might have been fucking around while she was here. I didn't pay her that much attention, to be honest. Anyway, she had it for sure when she came back, and died from it after a bit, but not before she had gone quite mad."

I did not say so aloud, but I was not sure that the rest of the family was so very far from that state either. Whether it was from the pox or not, I could not guess.

"Ellen never forgave her family, and Branston in particular," Win said. "Or maybe it was her mother she could not forgive."

Which made Ellen's bitterness more understandable, but I sensed something else under that pent up anger, however, a rather sad vulnerability. I hoped that someone someday would get through to her, but I felt sorry at the same time for the one who finally did. She was not a particularly likable person, and I did not imagine that she would ever be pleasant to live with.

Only once was there any suggestion of intimacy between Ellen and myself, and when that did happen, it was of the sort that I might well have predicted, the family being how they were.

I decided one evening that I did not feel in the mood to read. The book on farming was not exactly exciting, although I did fancy I was learning a bit. I supposed on this occasion that everyone else was watching television in the front room, and Branston, I thought, was in his office. I let myself out the front door and paused to stare up at the night-time sky, so clear here that you almost felt you could reach up and pluck a handful of those stars twinkling overhead. It was warm, but there was a gentle breeze blowing. The night air was perfumed. I was beginning to recognize the scents by now: honeysuckle, and jasmine, the roses from the garden.

It was a minute or two before I realized I was not alone. Someone was sitting at the top of the steps. I looked more closely and recognized the white dress Ellen had been wearing at dinner. She had said nothing when I came out, though she could hardly be unaware of my presence.

"Ellen?" I asked.

"Were you expecting Venus?" she said. "No, wait, she was Roman, wasn't she? Cytherea?"

"Aphrodite, I think you mean," I said. I came to sit beside her. "No, it is just that you were so quiet, I thought for a minute you might be a ghost."

"Maybe I am," she said. "Maybe we all are. You have to admit, the Rawleys seem a bit insubstantial, don't they?" Her tone was as cool as usual, but she moved over to make room for me on the steps.

"Unhappy, I think is the word," I said.

"Yes. I am, certainly," she agreed. "Miserably unhappy and too lazy or too weak to do anything about it. We all are. There you have it, that's the Rawleys in a nutshell." She paused, and added, with a dry laugh, "A nutshell. Now there's a perfect description for us. What about you, little Greek boy? Are you unhappy here?"

I shrugged. "Not as much as I thought I would be," I said. "When I first came, I mean. I guess if I really considered it, I would have to say I am happy enough."

"Really?" She sounded surprised. She looked hard at me. "I suppose Leticia has found a way to molest you?"

"Why do you say that?" I stammered.

"Oh, I know Leticia, she'd have got what she wanted if she had to tie you down. And my dear Daddy, too, no doubt," she said. "Let me see, that leaves me and Branston, doesn't it? You needn't worry about him, boys aren't his thing. I know, because once a week, as regular as clockwork, he blesses me with his divine rod. I suppose the rest of the time he relies on a five fingered lover."

Her remark startled me. "You mean, you and Branston....?"

"Don't look so surprised," she said, giving me the ghost of a smile. "That's why he hates me so much. I am the only one permitted to see him as a human being. Or something very like a human being, anyway, although what Branston really is, is a ten inch cock with a six and half foot appendage fastened to it so it can get around."

I was speechless at this news. Except for my own fantasies, and I knew them for what they were, I had never envisioned Branson having sex with anyone. To be honest, I was disappointed, too. It seemed as if my God had a crotch of clay.

My surprises were not over for the night, however. Ellen leaned toward me in the darkness and put a hand on my leg. "I suppose I might as well uphold our family tradition, and have my way with you too," she said. "We could do it here, if you like, al fresco. Branston's out to the barn on some errand, and Win and Leticia never come out here after dark. They have got too many ghosts."

"What do you mean?" I asked stupidly.

She moved her hand up toward my crotch. "I should think that would be evident," she said, "Or am I too repulsive for you to fuck, Greek boy?"

"No, you are not repulsive," I stammered. "Only...."

I did not want to explain to her where my tastes lay. Luckily, I was saved the necessity of further explanation. We heard the barn door slam in the distance. Ellen jerked her hand away from my leg as if it had been burned and, a moment later, Branston appeared out of the gloom.

Ellen jumped up without a word or a glance at me, and disappeared into the house, the screen door banging loudly behind her. Branston paused, and looked after her, and then gave me a penetrating glance. I blushed, but I managed to meet his eyes.

After a moment, he went past me into the house. "It's late, boy," was all he said as the door banged closed again.

THE GREEK BOY, BY VICTOR J. BANIS

◉ CHAPTER SIX ◉

For a time after Ellen had told me about her sexual connection with Branston, I wondered if maybe she had been making it up. I might as well confess, I wanted to think that she had, but logically, I could not think of any reason why she should. Probably, my refusal to believe was as much a question of jealousy, as anything. I resented knowing that someone else was having the pleasures of his sexuality that I myself wanted so badly, never mind the futility of my desire.

Oddly, it was only a few nights after our conversation on the front steps that something occurred which confirmed what she had said, and convinced me that she was right about why the two of them hated one another so vehemently. In their use of one another, they revealed to themselves the truth of their sexual needs, which no amount of personal dislike had been able to negate.

My discovery of this came about entirely by accident. Unable to sleep one night, I tossed and turned on my bed for some time, which only aggravated my sleeplessness, and finally I gave up and went downstairs, thinking that I would find something in the library to read. There was moonlight enough to see my way down the stairs and I left the lights out, not wanting to wake anyone else.

The door to the library was almost but not quite closed, and I was nearly there before I saw the dim light shining through the scant opening. I thought at first that someone had just forgotten to put the light out earlier, but before I quite got to the door I heard voices, speaking low, and I paused. I quickly realized that one of the voices was Branston's deep basso. It took me a moment to recognize that the other was Ellen's.

The proper thing for me to have done, of course, was to turn around and go back to my room, since the late hour and the almost closed door were enough to suggest that whatever conversation they were having was meant to be private, and certainly I had no business eavesdropping. At the very least, I should have coughed or made some sound to let them know I was there.

I did neither. I confess, shameful though it might be, I was overcome with curiosity, and I came toward the door with deliberate stealth. The opening was so slight that I felt sure they would not see me in the darkness outside, while when I leaned close to the opening and looked through it, I found that they were as visible to me as if they were on a lighted stage.

From the tone of their voices and the expressions on their faces, it was immediately clear that they were quarreling. Ellen wore a faded pink robe, loosely tied at the waist, her hair tousled as if she had come from bed, and Branston was naked except for those tight white trousers he wore to work in. I saw him naked from the waist up every day while we worked, of course, but this time I could stare unabashedly at that broad chest and those thick muscled shoulders and arms, and I feasted my eyes on that manly beauty in a way that I could not when he was aware of my presence. I saw, too, that his trousers were unbelted, and the fly half open, to reveal a patch of red-gold hair in the v that was formed there. I think it was this, as much as anything, that kept me glued to my watching post. This was as close as I had ever gotten to seeing his crotch, and that little bit of spun gold hypnotized me.

Something he said had riled her and she gave me a real scare when she jumped up from the chair she had been sitting in and started toward the door. "I am sick of you and your insults," she snapped at him. "I am going to bed."

I jumped and half turned to flee, but it turned out to be unnecessary.

"You are not going anywhere," he said. His voice was calm and smooth, unlike hers. Whatever the situation was, and I had not yet sorted it out, it was obvious that he was in total control of it, and she knew that as well, to her anger. She stopped dead in her tracks and threw him a furious look.

"You despise me as much as I despise you, Branston," she said sharply. "Why do you even want me, is what I would like to know?"

A rare grin crossed his face, but it was not a pretty or a friendly one. "Well, shit, Ellen," he said in a mocking tone, "A man has got to get himself a piece of ass every once in a while, doesn't he? It keeps everything in working order, so things don't get all rusted up. Besides, let's don't kid ourselves, darling, you need steady fucking same as I do. You would plain go crazy if you didn't get yourself some prick. If I didn't take care of business for you, why, you would be sniffing around for somebody else's, and it wouldn't much matter whose. So, you could say, I am doing it for the family's honor, lest you end up in the bushes with that pecker-headed mailman."

Despite the insulting nature of his remarks, she made no further attempt to leave, only stood and watched him with eyes that filled with hatred, but with something else that I recognized soon enough.

He came to where she waited and stood close behind her, and one enormous hand came around and slipped under her faded chenille robe, moving down across her belly.

"I'll kill you some day," she said, but her voice had lost its sting. His fingers had already found their goal and she had begun to breath faster. She leaned back against him, and closed her eyes, her nostrils flaring.

"No you won't, Ellen, not so long as the big hairy one is there to take care of things for you," he said. He tugged the robe free and it fell to the floor at their feet. Naked, she turned to him, her arms coming up around him, and he leaned down to kiss her. After a moment, he bent slightly and lifted her into his powerful arms as easily as if she weighed no more than a feather. In three long strides he had carried her to the sofa and laid her on it with surprising gentleness.

I almost fainted in the next moment, as I realized he was undoing the rest of the buttons on his fly, and one hand tugged downward at his trousers. I was going to see him naked, just as I had so often dreamed of doing. The thought of it excited me so that my knees threatened to buckle under me and I had to support myself with a hand on the doorjamb.

The trousers fell about his feet. For a brief instant I thought he was wearing shorts under them, but it was only the stark white of his ass in contrast to the deep brown of his back. An ass that was everything I had dreamed it to be, deliciously curved mounds so firm they looked carved of alabaster, and that deep secret valley between them that I longed to explore with my tongue.

He half turned for a moment and for the first time I finally saw the prick of my dreams, standing out before him in all its glory. Ten inches, Ellen had said, and she had not exaggerated, a long thick shaft and a big, ruby colored head with a drop of dew already glistening at its tip. My tongue moved instinctively, wanting to suck up that gleaming droplet, and I swallowed hard, my throat dusty dry with desire. His massive balls swayed like hairy pendulums as he moved quickly to step out of his trousers. My own cock began to grow inside my pants and all unconsciously I reached down to rub its swelling length.

Ellen's legs were spread for him and I could see that she was already wet with welcome for his stiff rod. He lowered himself atop her, turned away from me, so that I had a perfect view of his butt, that downy valley spread wide now, his balls swinging ponderously as he positioned himself. I watched him grasp his thick, hard shaft in one hand and guide the knob to the opening, burying it within her and, without a pause, shoving it home.

She moaned aloud as he thrust deeply into her, and her legs came up around him. One thing was blatantly obvious: whatever the rest of her thought of him, her pussy certainly loved what he rammed into her. Beneath him, she twisted and pushed upward to welcome him. The moisture that dripped out of her and dampened his balls gleamed in the lamplight and she made little animal noises as she clung to him. Down and up he went, down and up, his balls slapping against her upturned butt. The muscles in his back and ass tightened, relaxed, tightened, relaxed, his little hole winking invitingly at me with each thrust. Each time he pulled back I could see the whole length of him, wet with her juices, before it disappeared into her again.

He was riding her harder and faster, really ramrodding her now. She grew more frantic with each violent poke, jerking and groaning and clawing at his naked back until her nails left bloody marks on his shoulders.

I was nearly as frantic by this time as she was. I yanked my throbbing cock out of my pants and began to jerk off violently, not even caring if they heard, though of course they were too busy with their own activities to take any notice of me. In my imagination, it was not her, but me, that he was riding so furiously.

Her movements grew even more frenzied as her climax neared, but my eyes were glued to Branston, watching for the telltale signs of his orgasm. I saw him slam it into her up to the balls with a bone jarring thrust, twisting his hips as to give her everything he had. He grunted, the muscles in his ass cheeks grew taut and his butthole began to spasm tightly. I knew he was coming deep inside her, and the thrill of knowing that was happening brought my own load erupting out of me. It splashed against the doorjamb and onto the carpet. I slapped a hand over my mouth to stifle the moan that nearly erupted as ell, and leaned against the wall, gasping for breath and too numb even to think for a moment.

Branston's swollen prick, crimson red and drenched with love juices, hers and now his too, slipped out of her, and he moved back from her and started to get up from the sofa.

Frightened, I grabbed my handkerchief from my back pocket and hastily wiped up most of my come from the door and the carpet, before I ran for the stairs, not even taking time to put my dangling cock away. I avoided the banister and the rickety newel post at the top, lest they creak and reveal the truth to the man downstairs. Not until I had reached the safety of the floor above did I pause to shove it back into my trousers.

I could already hear him climbing the stairs as I slipped hastily into my room. I closed my door quietly and leaned against it, catching my breath and listening to his footsteps as they passed in the hall.

I only wished I had the courage to offer to lick him clean with my tongue.

* * * * * * *

In the days that followed, I was haunted by the images of Branston naked, his cock hard, his eyes flashing with lust. Whenever I was around him, which was a great deal of the time now, those erotic pictures superimposed themselves over the reality of the moment, and I seemed to see him as I had seen him that night.

The difficulty was that, the moment those lurid images entered my mind, my body began automatically to respond. My blood would race, my temples throb—and of course my dick would start to swell. For nearly a week I was almost constantly at least half hard, and sometimes more than that, whenever I was with him, and it taxed my ingenuity to find ways to keep it concealed from him. He must surely have wondered why I talked to him so much of the time with my back turned.

I remained puzzled, though, by the animosity that he and Ellen had displayed for one another, their sexual heat notwithstanding. She hated him, it was clear, and he seemed no fonder of her.

It was not just her, either, as I came to realize. They all hated him, Leticia and Win as much as Ellen, and he hated them equally. Of course, even I could see that the family was eccentric, and all of them were sexually deranged. But Branston was not exactly a monk himself; I knew that now for myself. Anyway, I felt sure that he had sowed plenty of wild oats while he had been roaming about the country. A man did not learn to fuck like that without plenty of experience.

I was sure that there was something more than just their sexual foibles that had wounded him to the very center of his being, something that must have driven him away all those years ago. Whatever it was, the poison was still in him, in all of them, still festering.

As people will, I puzzled over these matter without considering that the simplest way to get answers is quite often simply to ask for them.

The answers, some of them at least, came on a Sunday. Our routine was different on Sundays. For one thing, it was Mrs. Corey's day off, which meant that we had a lighter breakfast than was the custom, usually reheated biscuits and gravy, and sometimes to my surprise, Branston himself fried up some leftover potatoes or some sausages, and I found those particularly to my liking, all the more delicious because I knew that he had prepared them. No one else, it seemed, made any effort to cook.

After breakfast, we went to church, all of us. That was another of Branston's edicts. He drove the station wagon, Leticia in the front seat beside him, and Win and Ellen and I crowded into the back, and we rode in silence all the way to the Methodist Church in Rawley's Landing.

I had attended church regularly with my mother back in Greece, so I was accustomed to the Greek Orthodox service, with all its pomp and trappings. This was strange to me, but not unpleasant. For one thing, I got to see other people for a change, which was pleasant after the isolation of the farm. I saw, too, that, like Mister Willford and his clerks at the clothing store, the locals treated the Rawleys as aristocracy. They were courteous to us, but careful to keep a certain distance. A few men shook Branson's hand, and if Leticia happened to smile at one of the women, the smile was quickly returned. Ellen was as silent and aloof as she always was. I noticed that one or the other of the men took notice of her, but she ignored them steadfastly, neither speaking to nor looking directly at anyone. Win spoke to many men and women both, and they returned his greetings or comments, though I quickly realized they were not so friendly as when he and I had been in town alone.

I was an object of curiosity, needless to say, and people stole little glances when they thought they would not be too conspicuous, which I pretended not to notice. Several of the young women noticed me, which made me think that probably there were not a lot of available young men in town; and one handsome dark haired fellow not much older than myself gave me a look that made me feel Win and I were not alone in our leanings. I smiled warmly at him and looked away before he could get too encouraged; and lest Branston notice and guess what it was all about. When the next hymn began, I sang with particular fervor.

After church, we went home for lunch, usually cold cuts and potato salad or coleslaw, which was new to me and which I rather favored. When we had eaten lunch, Branston and Leticia went out again, still dressed up, to pay visits to the locals. One Sunday each month, Branston went alone to visit the tenant farmers—sharecroppers, Leticia called them scornfully—but for those visits he changed out of his dark suit and went in his work clothes.

On the Sunday after I had witnessed that erotic but bizarre scene between Branston and Ellen, we went to church as usual. He and Leticia were quarreling over something the subject of which was unknown to me, and both to and from church they sniped at one another, though I had no clue what it was all about.

After lunch, Branston got ready to go visiting as usual, but Leticia seemed set on remaining where she was, in a rocker on the porch.

"It's time we were going," he told her pointedly when she continued to linger.

"Maybe I do not feel like going," she said, with a rare show of independence. "Maybe I just get fed up with traipsing around the countryside to make boring conversation with people I do not much care for to begin with."

"Maybe you had best change your mind," he said in a cold, hard voice. "Maybe you will be all ready to go in ten minutes. I am sure it is boring for you, Leticia. It is not particularly exciting for me, I can damn well tell you, but we are going anyway, both of us, in the station wagon, in no more than ten minutes from now."

For a second or two I thought she meant to defy him; but she had not that much spirit, or else it deserted her in the face of his anger. Without looking in his direction, she got up and hurried into the house. They left together shortly, the station wagon jouncing down the drive, in well under Branston's ten-minute deadline.

Ellen had gone up to her own room immediately after lunch, so Win and I were left alone on the porch when the station wagon had disappeared down the drive in a cloud of dust.

"Why does he hate her so?" I asked, looking after them. "All of you? He seems to hate the whole family, and all of you to hate him as well. But why?"

"We're Rawleys," he said. "That's enough reason for him to hate us, I guess. And I suppose we are just returning the favor."

"But he is a Rawley, too. And he seems to think the family name is so important. And he works so hard to make a go of things here. It makes no sense to me."

Win thought a minute. "I guess it is about his father, as much as anything. I know for certain he would never have come back here while his father was still alive, or Leticia's husband, either. He hated both of them with a fury."

It was a moment before I realized what he had said. "You mean Leticia's husband was not Branston's father?" I asked.

"Well, now, see, I had completely forgotten you wouldn't know about that." He paused and I had a feeling he was debating about whether he should say more or not. "Leticia is Branston's mother, as you already know, but they are not just mother and son. They are brother and sister, too. They had the same father. Do you understand what I am saying?"

"I do not think I do understand," I said, puzzling over it. "You can not mean that, Leticia and…and her own father…?"

He gave me a mocking grin. "Now, don't tell me you have never heard of such a thing. Isn't there one of those old Greek stories along the same lines?"

"Oedipus, yes," I said, "But that...well, that is different."

"So are the Rawleys," he said. "'sides, you would have to have known old Jess, Leticia's father, that is. He was a Rawley through and through, by which I mean to say that his pecker could not ever get enough pussy. He was a lot like Branston, too, a real bastard, but a god to look at. And the way he was, if he wanted something, he took it, and to hell with what anyone else thought or wanted. And he was even worse than Branston when it came to family. The thing was, he had his heart set on seeing the family name handed down to a worthy heir. That was what he wanted more than anything else in the world, a grandson with the Rawley name."

"But what about you?" I asked. "You were married. Could he not have waited for you to produce an heir for him?"

"Me?" Win gave a sad snort of a laugh. "I wasn't ever enough of a man to please him. It was not my offspring he wanted. He wanted Leticia's. She was beautiful, understand, you just cannot imagine, seeing her now, how beautiful she was when she was young, and headstrong and clever, she had all the family traits. Including the hot pants, as you already know. He could see by the time she was seventeen that she was not likely to wait much longer to start getting it somewhere. So, what he did, he went and picked out a husband for her and got her married off, and he even got her husband to adopt the Rawley name, so their child when it came would be a Rawley."

"Well, then?" I said.

"It just didn't go the way he figured, was what it was," Win said. "The trouble was, as much as he thought he knew about men, he picked the wrong one for a husband for Leticia. He just was not any match for Leticia's sexual appetites, once they had been aroused. Once a month was a about his speed, and that was about twenty-nine times a month fewer than Leticia had been counting on. Worse than that, even, was that after a year of trying, nothing had come of it. So, Jess set them down at the table one evening and he told them out plain that he was getting impatient for a grandson. And when that still did not have any results, he sent them

90

both up north, to Cincinnati, to a clinic, to see if there was some problem. As it turned out, there was. It didn't make any difference how often they did it or for how many years, her husband was never going to get any babies growing in Leticia. He didn't have the right kind of seed, it seemed like."

"And that is why Leticia's father—but surely he did not want a grandson that badly?" I said, scarcely able to believe what he was telling me.

"I told you, once old Jess had his mind set on something he was going to have it, come hell or high water, and he had his mind set on Leticia's giving him a grandson. Besides, he was not a man to concern himself about any kind of morality, or what other people might think was right or wrong. If he wanted it, then it was right, to his way of thinking. Well, the long and short of it was, she did get pregnant, all right, not long after that trip up to the clinic, when they had learned the truth of things. The way I heard it, the old man got himself tanked up one night on his favorite bourbon, went up to their bedroom bold as brass, and told her husband to get his sorry ass out of bed and let a real man do the job."

I thought for a moment of what an ugly story it was. "I can see how Branston would hate his father so," I said, "But why should he hate Leticia so for what happened? She was innocent, surely. If her father was that determined...."

He snorted again. "I don't know that I would ever have described Leticia as innocent, now or then. I told you, she had a hot bottom on her, and she wasn't too happy being stuck with that weak-spined man her Daddy had picked out for her, and who was not doing her much good. And her Daddy was a gorgeous looking man. I reckon you have seen that picture of him on the stairs, and he had a whopper on him that would have put a horse to shame. Hell, it had kept smiles on the faces of a great many women around the county for years.

"The upshot of all this was, Leticia booted her husband out of their bedroom for good that same night, and even though nobody talked about it, her Papa spent most of his nights after that in hers. He liked a good piece of ass, and his own wife was frail and not much use for that sort of thing, I imagine. She spent most of her time laying abed and sipping juleps. Anyway, it was not long after that at all that Leticia announced one morning at the breakfast table that she was going to have a baby. Her husband loaded up the shotgun that same day and took it with him out to the barn and blew his head clear off. Didn't seem to me like anyone grieved much for him, either. I don't think Leticia or her Daddy hardly noticed he was gone."

I felt embarrassed and shocked by the story I had heard. We Greeks were pretty liberal when it came to sexual matters but even to me this sounded disgusting. "How could a man even think about screwing his own daughter?" I wondered aloud.

Win gave me a peculiar look and stood up, but as he went into the house, he said, "Depravity just seems to come natural to the Rawleys, hadn't you noticed?"

◙ CHAPTER SEVEN ◙
▲

I was so new to all this, that I forgot that the farm was so old. And the Rawleys went back for many generations, so it was understandable that I forgot that, in a sense, Branston himself was nearly as much a newcomer as I was. He had left here, from what Win told me, when he was only fifteen years old, just a boy, really, and he had stayed away for twenty years. It had not been more than two years since he had returned.

Which is a roundabout way of saying that what I thought of as a long time situation was really a fairly recent one, and one that, in the next few days, came to a head. It was inevitable, considering the hatred that existed between Ellen and Branston, that sooner or later the ugly sparks of her resentment would eventually burst into flames. It was just a little over two weeks after I saw the two of them in the library together that I witnessed another emotionally charged scene between them.

I had tiptoed downstairs often during the night, hoping for a repeat performance in the library, but I never found them there again. I remembered what Ellen had said originally: once a week. But if they did it the following week, they must have found another place to do it than the library. Or maybe one of the other of them had actually known about my spying on them. Would either of them have said anything? Ellen, perhaps not; but, Branston—could he have known, and taken some kind of pleasure in being observed. I would like to have thought so—but I had not the nerve to ask.

On this occasion, however, Branston and Ellen were not sexually engaged, and I did not have to watch them surreptitiously from outside the library door. When trouble flared up, it happened at the table, while we were just finishing dinner, and we were all of us witnesses.

I could see all the way through that dinner that something was afoot, though I had no clue what. Ellen was even more distant than usual, and at the same time she had a strange air about her: anticipation, I thought, even triumph. For his part, Branston, though he had been pleasant enough at work in the fields with me, had grown even more than usually sullen. Something was there, between the two of them—but what?

It was not until Mrs. Corey had removed the last of the dinner dishes and served the coffee, after which she always went home, that Branston finally addressed Ellen directly.

"I am told you went into town today," he said. The question surprised me. I would have said that no one in the family went anywhere without his permission.

"Yes," she said simply, her attention focused entirely on her cup of coffee. She added sugar to it, spoon after spoon, four in all, and then stirred it slowly, apparently fascinated by the swirling liquid. She added nothing to that monosyllable.

Not to be dissuaded, Branston pursued the subject. "Had you some purpose for this trip," he asked, "Other than to waste gasoline?"

"I went to see Doctor Bromley," she said. "As you must perfectly well know. Since someone saw fit to tell you about the trip," she looked angrily around at the others, but everyone avoided her glance, "I am sure they must have told you the reason as well."

"Yes, I was told it was to see the doctor," Branston said, "But I was not told why. Have you not been well?"

Later, I thought that perhaps Branston already knew why. I do not know how he might have known, but the man seemed to know everything concerning the farm and his family, so that it would not have surprised me.

She took a long time to answer, having once again become fascinated by the coffee in her cup, though she had yet to take a sip of it. Finally, she took a deep breath, and screwed up her courage enough to fling out at him, "I'm pregnant."

Leticia set her cup down with such a bang I was surprised the saucer did not shatter. Win only sat frozen, gaping at his daughter. As for Branston, he stared in silence at her, and I looked from him to Ellen and back again in anxious confusion.

"Whose it is?" Branston asked finally, in a voice like ice.

She looked at him with surprise and—I could not help but see—amusement. "There is no point in our pretending, Branston," she said. "Everybody at this table knows you have been fucking me regular."

She waited for his reply. When it did not come, when he only sat and stared at her with that blank face of his, she began to look nervous again, but she pressed on. "I don't care for you any more than you care for me, Branston, and we are cousins, but it does look like you will have to marry me, unless you want your son to be born a bastard. Which means that the Rawley name will go on, it seems. Isn't that nice to think? It will be our little son who will inherit all of this in time."

He was silent for so long that you could have cut the tension about the table with a knife. "You filthy whore," he said finally, spitting the words at her. "Do you take me for some kind of a fool?" He grinned at her, but it was a terrifying sight. "I knew all along that you were a cock-sucking slut, but I swear to God, Ellen, I actually thought if I fucked you regularly till you couldn't walk, I could keep you satisfied and out of mischief. I didn't though, did I? One stiff prick wasn't enough to keep you happy, apparently."

She jumped suddenly to her feet and ran around to his end of the table, and dropped to her knees beside his chair. "It was, Branston, I swear it was." She began to cry, and clutched at his legs. "You were the only one, the whole time, just you. I don't care how much you hate me, you can't change the truth. You are my baby's father, and nobody else."

He shoved her away, so violently that she fell on her back on the floor. "I guess I could have told you," he said, standing abruptly. He bumped the table, setting the china to rattle. "You can have all the babies you want, Ellen, but they will not be mine. Not this one, not any of them. I am not ever going to plant any babies, not in you, and not in any other woman."

"It is yours, Branston," she shouted, but she cringed and tried to crawl backward away from him, away from his anger. "The baby is yours. I swear it."

He smiled that ugly smile again. "You swear? Well, I once swore, too, Ellen. I swore to myself, when I left here, I swore I would never be to blame for bringing another Rawley into this world. And I saw to it that I would never renege on that promise just because I had hot nuts for someone. There are ways that can be guaranteed, things a doctor can do to a man. You've looked at my balls up close plenty of times, Ellen; you have slobbered all over them and felt them up plenty good. Didn't you ever notice that little bitty scar at the back of them?"

"Scar? I don't know what you're talking about." She stopped crying as suddenly as she had begun, and her voice was almost normal sounding. "What scar?"

"The doctor cut me," he said coldly, "Where a man's sperm comes out. I have been fixed. You talk to Doctor Bromley. Talk to anybody you like, they will all tell you the same thing. I couldn't make a baby, Ellen, not in a million years."

She gaped open-mouthed, and looked directly into his eyes. Whatever she saw there must have convinced her he was telling the truth, though, or maybe she knew him well enough to know that this was not the sort of thing he would make up. She got to her feet, as calm all of a sudden as if they had been discussing the weather, her own face as expressionless as his was. She took a moment to brush off her skirt, not even looking at him, and walked around him—I give her credit, she went by him without flinching. With the wrath in his face, I do not think I could have done that, but she was now as cool as a cucumber. She went to the sideboard against the wall and poured herself a glass of sherry from the decanter that sat there, and took a small sip of it.

"I asked you before," he said, "Whose is it?"

"I have got no idea," she said. After all the violent emotion of the last several minutes, she seemed to have entirely lost her fear of him. When she turned around to face him again, she looked completely calm, even amused again.

"What do you mean, you have got no idea?" he asked. "You must know who you fucked. Didn't you even ask him his name?"

She smiled at him, a smile that dripped venom, it seemed to me. "Well, since you want to know, Branston," she said, "The way it happened was, I was walking alongside the road one afternoon, I was picking some wildflowers, I thought I would put them in my hair, for your benefit, and these two fellows, young fellows, not much more than boys, I reckon, came by in a car, and they stopped, and asked me did I want a ride, and I said, wouldn't they like to have a ride instead, and they said, why, sure they would, all giggling and winking at one another, and I got in the car with them, and we went down the road a ways and parked in the ditch. We got out of the car and we went behind some bushes there, where you couldn't be seen from the road. I can show you the place, if you would like. It's very private, just perfect for fucking of an afternoon. And that is what we did. I fucked them both. One of them twice, on account of he sort of reminded me of you, Branston."

I could see he was restraining his temper with an effort. I saw his fists clench and unclench at his side, and was half afraid that he might hit her. "What were their names?" he asked.

She tossed her head. "I didn't ask. This was not a social engagement, you understand. I didn't think the usual rules of etiquette applied, under the circumstances"

He was silent for a moment, glaring at her. "Were they the only two?" he asked finally.

She laughed softly. "Would it make you feel better if I said that they were? It isn't true, but I will say it, if it will make you feel any better."

"Who else?" he asked through clenched teeth. "How many?"

"I don't rightly know how many there were," she said with a shrug. "I told them, those two boys, when we were finished, I said if they had any friends wanted some pussy, tell them to come to that same spot about two o'clock of an afternoon, I would be there most days if it was not raining."

"And they came?"

"Yes, just about every day, sometimes there would be just one all by his lonesome, and sometimes there would be three or four of them. What I told myself every time, was, I would do it just until I found the one who was better than you, Branston, the one who could make me forget what it was like with you riding me, inside me. And when I did, when I found that one, I promised myself I would come home and tell you that you were not getting it any more, and I would laugh in your face." She shook her head and a sad, faraway look came into her eyes. "I never did find one that good, though. I tried, honestly, I tried, just about every day this summer, man after man, time after time. But I never found him. I am sorry to say, none of them even came close."

I was so hypnotized by the drama being played out before me that I did not realize that Branston had turned to me, was staring at me with those amethyst eyes glinting sparks. When I realized, I jumped and turned white as a ghost.

"Did you fuck her too?" he asked.

"Yes, he did," Ellen lied quickly, spitefully. I could not trust my voice, but I shook my head hard and stared straight at him, into his eyes, and he seemed to believe what he saw in mine. He turned on Win.

"Did you?" he demanded coldly.

Win was so terrified that he did not even try to lie. "Only two times, Branston," he stammered, "I swear, that was all. I was drunk both times, I swear it, that was all there was."

98

Branston said something, so low I could not hear it. He rubbed the back of his hand across his eyes and for a moment I almost thought he was crying, but he was perfectly cool and calm when he spoke to Ellen again.

"You will leave this house tomorrow," he said. "I do not want to see you here ever again."

"What am I supposed to live on?" she asked.

He gave her a withering look. "Maybe you can sell some of that pussy you have been giving around. Or maybe you can trick one of those peckerheads into marrying you. Frankly, I don't give a rat's ass. You will not get a red cent out of this place."

She looked hard at him, and Leticia, and finally, ignoring me as if I were not there, she turned to Win. "Say something, why don't you," she said, "You are my father, aren't you?"

"Don't expect anything from him, either," Branston said before Win could reply. "He won't help you, not as long as he is living under this roof. If he does, he will go with you. I told you, not a red cent."

Win looked at his daughter and gave a helpless shrug. She looked at him with brutal scorn.

I will give her credit: she had guts. She might have pleaded or argued with Branston, though even I knew he was not likely to change his mind once he had made it up, not on something this major. Her face went white and I saw tears forming in her eyes again, but she thrust her chin up and went by him, out of the room, without another word. The stairs creaked as she went up them.

Branston picked up the decanter of sherry then, and giving vent, finally, to the fury within him, he flung it against the wall. It shattered, shards of crystal and rivulets of sherry raining down upon the carpeted floor. Wordlessly, he strode from the room, and a moment later, the door of the library slammed closed.

Ellen was gone by the time I came down for breakfast.

* * * * * * *

Despite the fact that she had lied to Branston and tried to get me in trouble, I felt bad about Ellen, and I wished that I could help her, but there was not really anything I could do. I had no money to give her, and no way of sending her food or anything else she might need. We had not been friendly, but I would gladly have tried to give her moral support, at least. I could not even venture into Rawley's Landing, however, without Branston's permission, and I knew better than to ask him for that.

I was amazed, though, that Leticia and Win seemed, from the day she left, to forget that she had ever existed. No one mentioned her name, and so far as I know, neither of them pleaded her case with Branston, and if they gave her any financial help, it was secret indeed.

Once, I ventured to bring the subject up with Win. I asked him if he knew how she was. We were alone, but he looked over his shoulder as if he was afraid someone might hear.

Instead of answering my question, he asked one of his own: "What makes you ask that?" he wanted to know.

"She is family," I said, and was tempted to add, "She is your daughter," but I did not.

"She is living in town, above the dry goods store," he said, and walked away before I could ask for any more details. I wondered if she were paying her rent in the manner Branston had suggested, but if she were, I doubted that Win would tell me, if he even knew.

I did see her one time, but only at a distance. I was with Branston, and we had driven into town. It was not by any special invitation that I went with him. He did not say, as I fantasized, "Spiro, my love, I must go into town and you must come with me because I cannot bear to be parted from you."

It was just that the battery in the station wagon had died, and he had to drive into Rawley's Landing to buy a new one, and as I was with him in the field, it was simpler for him to take me with him than to drive me back to the house, so I rode along in the pickup, glad for the break in our routine.

100

We got the battery at the Sinclair filling station at the edge of town. I found the place fascinating, as it was something new to me. We had service stations in Greece, of course, but since I had never had any connection with motorcars, I had never spent any time at one.

I watched the attendant man the two pumps that stood outside, fascinated by the whirling numbers in the gauges, and inside, another man lay on his back on a low trolley and slid in and out under a car. There was an elevator of sorts onto which you could drive an automobile and which then could lift it into the air so that its underside could be studied and serviced. Everything was permeated with the smell of gasoline and oil and old grease, and there was a calendar on the wall in the repair area that showed a big-busted woman in a skimpy outfit.

The fact that the two uniformed attendants who worked there were both young, male and attractive might have had some bearing on my fascination. Branston, of course, took no notice of that, but I watched them out of the corner of my eye and was reminded once again of my current state of celibacy.

As it happened, it would take some time for the sandy haired attendant—my pick of the two—to charge the battery up for us. We went on into town while he did so, and had lunch at the counter at the bus depot. I had a hamburger again, and another of those malteds, and it seemed to me that they were even more delicious than they had been the previous time, probably because I was sitting at the counter next to Branston.

We talked very little as we ate—we talked very little most times, as far as that goes—but I found myself as usual hanging on every word that he said, and thrilling just to the sound of his deep baritone voice, softened as it was with the slightest of Southern drawls. Once, by the merest accident, his leg brushed against mine and lingered there. I almost dropped the glass with the malted in it, so electrified was I by the contact. I froze, unable to move, wanting so badly to increase the pressure where our legs touched, and knowing that I dared not. I felt an alarming heat in my crotch, and a faint stirring, and had a dreadful fear that I would very soon be sitting on that little stool with a full erection, and no way on earth that I could hide it.

I do not know if I was more relieved or heartbroken when he moved his leg after a moment, and the spell was broken. He, of course, had been totally unaware of it, and could have no idea what a clandestine thrill he had just given me, or that I would beat off twice that very night, remembering it.

We finished our lunch, I in a positive daze, and went back to the truck, and drove to pick up the new battery, and it was then that we saw Ellen, walking along the sidewalk on the opposite side of the street, going in the opposite direction. Or, at any rate, I saw her, but I cannot say with certainty whether he did or not.

"Oh," I said without thinking, "There is…" But I glanced sideways then, across the seat of the truck, and saw Branston's face, his eyes fixed straight ahead, his mouth set in a firm line, and I left the sentence unfinished, and only took a last, quick glance over my shoulder as she faded into the distance. I do not know if she saw us. If she did, she gave no more sign of it than Branston did.

To my great surprise, he mentioned her to me on the way home. "You think I was unfair to her?" he said, making a question of it. There was no need to say whom he meant. We both knew.

I thought about it for a long moment before I answered him. "I think what she did was shameful," I said finally. "It reflected badly on the family. On everyone. On you, especially." Which was not exactly an answer to the question he had asked, although he did not point that out. After another long moment, I ventured to add, "She must have been very much in love with you."

He glanced across at me, surprised. "Ellen? In love with me?" he said, "What makes you say a thing like that, boy?"

"Well, after all, the way she…" I had been about to say something about the way she had responded the night I watched him fuck her, and caught myself just in time. "The way she looked at you sometimes," I finished lamely instead.

He continued to look hard at me, as if he recognized the lie, but I was too embarrassed to even try to embellish it, and after a bit, he brought his attention back to the road, and said, "You must have seen it wrong. Looks can lie. The same as words"

I was tempted to say, her pussy did not lie, but I wisely kept that thought to myself.

THE GREEK BOY, BY VICTOR J. BANIS

◙ CHAPTER EIGHT ◙
▲

Branston and I had gotten friendlier as the days passed, although sadly it was only a distant kind of friendliness and not any real intimacy. At the same time, unfortunately, Win had gotten less friendly toward me.

Of course, I realized that most of the friendship between Win and me had to do with my cock, but he appeared to have even lost interest in that. I cannot say that I was altogether happy about this new disinterest on his part. I missed having a sexual outlet other than my own hand, which got plenty of regular exercise these days. Of course, I knew that I had only to hint to Leticia and she would be happy to provide me with relief, but that possibility had no appeal for me.

For that matter, I felt sure that I had only to hint to Win to end the drought, but I did not want him to think that I was in need. In any case, I doubt that Win would have continued for long to remain indifferent. He liked the taste of raw meat too well, and sooner or later he would have come around if only to satisfy his appetite. As it turned out, however, fate, and Branston, conspired to provide him an alternative dining treat.

Branston took on a hired hand.

I cannot in the least blame him for that, since God knows the help was needed. As hard as he worked, and as hard as I worked to help, Branston and I could only do so much. At the rate we were going, it would surely take us the entire rest of the summer just to finish clearing the trees from the backfield.

Branston got the idea, however, of adding some sheep to our livestock, and before he could do that, he would need to fence in a bit of pasture for them. Win had agreed that he could probably paint the fence when it was up, but there was no point in expecting him to build one, as he was no kind of a carpenter. Which meant that unless Branston was willing to take time away from our work out back, he had no choice but to hire someone to build him a fence.

The trouble was that he could not afford to pay much, and it took him a couple of weeks before he found someone who was available and competent to build a fence, and willing to work for what Branston offered.

"He ain't much, and he ain't bright," Branston told me frankly, in the way he had of sharing things with me that he did not speak of with the others. "But building a fence does not require a lot of brains. Anyway, I am told he is a good worker, just a little on the slow side."

For obvious reasons, I did not point out what Branston might not have noticed, not being so inclined, but that I had seen right off the bat—that the man he hired for the job was also young and reasonably good looking, in a crude sort of way. He was tall and slim, with sandy hair and freckles, and so long as he kept his mouth closed you did not see the badly stained teeth which otherwise marred his looks. What worried me more than his looks, though, was that he had an air about him that I recognized in an instant, having seen it in many other men in my past, and that told me he had a pair of hot nuts in those tight jeans he wore the first day he came to work, and would not be too particular about how they were taken care of. In Greece, we had a nickname for the type: Opoiodipote's. Anybody's. And that just about covered it.

It goes without saying, moreover, that with Branston and I chopping trees in the distant field and Leticia sternly forbidden even to speak to the young man unless she planned on moving into town with Ellen, Win was left alone with the new hand for most of the day. I had a sense of foreboding from the very first. I cannot say that the young man would have tempted me particularly. With my present lack of opportunities, I might have been tempted, but not tempted enough, I think, to do anything about it.

Like most of his family, however, Win was not very strong when it came to resisting temptation. He liked his cock, as I knew well enough, and he was not getting mine lately, and here, dropped right under his nose as it were, was a reasonably suitable candidate for getting himself some. And he must have spotted the availability as readily as I did.

I confess, at first I was puzzled that Branston felt safe in leaving them so alone, but when I thought some about it, I came to understand that Win had never given Branston any reason to worry about his behavior with men. I recalled how careful he had been with me to make certain Branston had no clue what were doing, and how insistently he had warned me against letting Branston find out about us. He had even waited for me to make the advances that first time, although he had not had much to worry about on that score, as I had made it pretty clear from the beginning that I was available. It just never occurred to me to think of Win taking an aggressive role, as frightened as he was of Branston and how Branston might react.

One thing I have long since learned about sucking cock, however; you can go without it for a long time and not miss it too much, but once you have had some, it kindles your appetite for more, an appetite that it is very difficult to sate. Win and I had had some hot sex together. I doubt that it was ever far from his mind now. And it was full summer by this time. Working in the hot sun next to an attractive, healthy young man, both of you shirtless, the sweat running, skin gleaming, firm young muscles flexing, it was not altogether surprising that Win's morals went to sleep. Truth was, they had never been particularly wide-awake to begin with.

What brought matters to a head was an incident that almost cost me mine. As Branston and I downed our trees, we trimmed them of branches and chopped and sawed the trunks and the larger branches into sections that we loaded in the truck and brought back over time to stack behind the barn—for firewood, Branston explained, which would cut back on heating bills when winter came.

I did most of this trimming and chopping. It was easier work than downing the trees, and I suspect that it was Branston's way of sparing me a bit, and I was grateful, and delighted by even this little evidence of his caring about me.

I was working on a really large tree on this particular day, only the second day that the new hand was working on the fence, when the blade suddenly came off my axe and sailed into the air. I was chopping so furiously that I did not even know what had happened till I heard Branston shout, "Look out, boy."

I ducked instinctively, or else the blade probably would have split my skull open. As it was, it barely grazed my arm, but Branston was there seconds later, grabbing hold of me by the shoulders and turning me back and forth.

"Are you all right?" he asked, and I was so thrilled by the concern evident in his eyes as he looked at me that I actually giggled and it fled my mind completely that I might have been killed.

I was all right, as it turned out. It was mostly the flat of the blade that had struck me, and I had a bad bruise there, and a cut on my arm from the edge of the blade where it had grazed me, but luckily not a deep one. Branston examined it as if it were life threatening, though, and washed it out with some tea from the thermos before he tore a piece off his shirt and wrapped it quickly around my arm, his powerful fingers surprisingly gentle.

I flexed my arm and said, "I think I can still work." Just at the moment, with all the attention and tender care he was showering on me, I would have been willing to work for him if the blade had taken my arm clear off, but he shook his head firmly.

"That will have to be taken care of," he said. "Anyway, the axe has got to be fixed. Shit, I ought to be horsewhipped for not noticing it was coming loose like that. You could have been hurt bad."

I thought that he had plenty enough to occupy his attention, and anyway, the axe's condition had not been obvious or I would have noticed it myself, but he did not want to hear any excuses from me. He loaded everything back into the truck, refusing when I tried to help and insisting instead that I go sit in the shade and rest my arm.

Everything was fine until we drove past the field where Win and the new man ought to have been working on the fence, but they were nowhere to be seen. The tools and the paint were there, and the boards for the fence, and there was more of the fence up than had been there at the beginning of the day, so they had done some work; but whatever the two of them were working on now, it was not a new fence.

Knowing Win as I did, I guessed right off what must of happened, and I tried frantically to think of some way to distract Branston from their absence, but he had already seen it for himself, and he had apparently drawn the same conclusion that I had.

"Damn it to hell," was all he said. He braked the truck to a skidding stop and jumped down without another word, all but running in the direction of the woods beyond the fence. I watched him go and tried to think how I could warn Win that trouble was on its way. I could honk the horn, of course, but Branston would hear that too, and I might only be making things worse—for myself, certainly. He could hardly not guess why I had done that.

One idea occurred to me: if I could find Win before Branston did, I might be able to avert certain disaster. I jumped down from the truck and ran for the woods myself, but taking a different path from the one Branston had taken.

I was no sooner in the woods, though, than I realized the futility of my plan. Win and Branston both knew these woods. Win would surely know just where to take someone for a little fun, and Branston would know just where to look for them, but I had no idea which way to run.

I plunged through the undergrowth regardless, bushes and twigs tearing at me, not daring to call Win's name, and the growth here was so thick that I almost ended up on top of him. I ran through some grass that was practically as tall as I was, and nearly plunged over an embankment that overlooked a small creek. I was able to grab the branch of a tree just in time to catch myself from going over.

The new hired man was standing directly below me. If I had fallen over the embankment, I would have landed right at his feet. He was leaning against a wide-trunked hickory tree with his dirty jeans down about his ankles and boxer shorts halfway there as well. Win knelt before him, and sucked energetically on a long, thin dick. The hired hand's face was turned up toward me and he would certainly have seen me if he had looked, but his eyes were closed and there was a happy smile on his face. It was clear he was enjoying the blowjob, but Win had sucked my dick before and I knew how skillful he could be.

I opened my mouth to call to Win, to warn him, but it was too late. The next minute Branston came crashing through some small bushes below, heedless of the noise he was making. The hired man heard him coming and, startled from his reverie, he opened his eyes wide to look in Branston's direction. Win heard him too and jerked away from the young man's hairy thighs, so abruptly that he almost toppled backwards into the creek behind him.

Branston took only a second or two to survey the scene. It did not take any great wits to see what was happening. He swore and ran at the half naked hired man, who bleated and tried to run and get his shorts and his jeans up all at the same time. He tripped and fell and the tip of Branston's boot caught him on his naked butt.

"I didn't do nothing," the young man sputtered, still trying to get away and get himself covered. "He made me do it, he told me I had to come back here and let him pleasure me if I wanted to keep the job."

"Get out," Branston ordered. "Don't even bother stopping for your money, I will see that you get that, never fear. I don't want to see you around here ever, you hear me. And don't you dare say nothing to anybody in town about this, unless you want to be the town queer, cause I will spread the word it was you sucking his cock."

"I didn't do nothing," the hired man insisted, but he staggered down the path, still struggling with his pants. "It weren't my fault, I tell you. He made me do it."

Win had gotten to his feet while this was going on and I half expected him to run too, but he stood motionless and watched white faced until Branston turned around to him.

"Don't hit me, Bran," Win said, and put up his hands up to protect himself, but Branston made no move toward him.

"A hired hand, Win?" Branston shouted. "Why in Jesus' name did you have to go and suck off a hired hand? He is the worst kind of white trash, that one, he can't read nor write even, that's how come I got him so cheap. I knew you were dick hungry but it never crossed my mind you would think of getting it off a piece of trash like that."

So, for all Win's caution, Branston did know about that, too. It did not greatly surprise me; he seemed to know his family's inclinations well. And what did he know about me, I wondered, but that question came to me later. For the moment, I was caught up in the drama below.

He was angry but as I stared down at Branston from my perch above them, I realized that there was more to it than mere anger. I suddenly saw that he was truly hurt by what Win had done. It was like Win had let him down, had broken his heart, even. Win seemed to sense that, too. "Bran," he started to say, and took a step in his direction, but Branston silenced him with a wave of his hand.

"Git," Branston said. "Go away, Win. Leave me be." He turned and leaned his cheek against the rough bark of the same tree that the young man had leaned against earlier. Win stared at him for a moment and actually took another step in his direction; but whatever he had considered, he thought better of it, and with a shrug, he followed his young swain down the path that led back to the house.

Up till this moment, no one had even noticed me standing on the little bluff. They had all been too involved in the drama they were enacting. If I had been smart, I would have gone, too, before Branston noticed me there; but I was moved by the sight of him, by the defeated slump I had never seen in his shoulders before, and the weary, pained expression on his face. I longed to run to him and comfort him.

I did not, of course, and after a moment, he looked up and saw me above him. I really was sorry now that I had not gone; I think realizing that I had witnessed the entire scene was harder for him than the scene itself had been. I tried to think of something I could say to lessen his obvious embarrassment, but my mind was a total blank.

He turned his back on me and started down the path. "We got that axe to fix, boy," he said, without looking back "And Leticia will need to see to that arm of yours."

I had forgotten entirely the wound on my arm. I followed the path to the house. Branston had been there before me, and Leticia was waiting. She washed the cut and put some iodine on it, which burned mightily, and put a fresh bandage over it. She gave me the scrap of Branston's shirt to throw in the trash, but when she looked away, I stuffed in it my pocket instead for a souvenir, remembering how concerned he had been.

When she had finished, I thanked her. "I'll go back to work now, I guess," I said, but she said, "Branston has already gone, I'm sure. I heard the truck just after you got here."

I went outside to see for myself, but the truck was gone, as she had said. He had already left without me, it seemed. I gave thought briefly to hiking back to the field, but it was a long walk and it would be almost time to quit before I got there. Anyway, I think he had made it clear that he did not want my company for the rest of the afternoon. I found chores to busy myself with about the barn and the house instead, and read for a bit in my room.

He was in his usual chair in the library when I came down before dinner, but he studiously ignored me and kept his attention fixed on his newspaper. I still could not think of anything to say that would make things comfortable for the two of us again. Leticia was there, sipping her glass of wine. I nodded at her and crossed the room to pour myself a glass of bourbon. While I was sipping it, I heard Win come in. I looked over my shoulder and was surprised to see that he was carrying a beat up old leather suitcase. He sat it on the floor at his feet and stood in the doorway, waiting for Branson to notice him.

When it became evident that Branston meant to ignore him as well, Win said, "I am leaving, Branston. Today.

Now. I am going to see if Ellen will let me stay with her till I get myself sorted out."

I looked at Branston, but Branston only continued to ignore him. When it became clear that Branston was not going to respond, Win picked up his suitcase again, and looked from me to Leticia. "When you two have had all you can take of Mister High and Mighty, here," he said, "You are welcome to come and see us in town." He turned and disappeared down the hall, and a moment later we heard the front screen door open and close behind him. I wondered if he meant to walk into town. It was a long walk, but I could hardly imagine Branston offering him the use of the car.

Branston did look up from his newspaper then. He stared hard at Leticia. "Are you planning on leaving as well?" he asked her, "Or will you be staying?"

She managed a sad looking smile for him. "I am not all that fond of ham and boiled potatoes," she said, "but they do fill a body up. Anyway, this is my home. I was raised here, and my Daddy, too, and his Daddy, for generations back. No, Branston, I am not leaving."

"Boy?" He looked at me.

"I do not have anywhere to go, sir," I said, and added, "Anyway, I like it here well enough. If you will let me stay, that is."

"I don't see anyone chasing you out," he said, and went back to his newspaper, to signal the end of the conversation. Leticia sat and sipped her wine. I emptied my glass of bourbon and filled it again.

Dinner was particularly quiet on that evening. Despite the drama of Win's leaving, it seemed as if no one had anything to say, and we all ate in silence and kept our attention focused on our plates. The atmosphere was weighted and sullen, and I was glad when, Branston having taken his leave with no more than a nod in Leticia's direction, I could flee to the sanctuary of the library.

* * * * * * *

In the days that followed, Branston was even more distant with me than he had been in the beginning. For better or for worse, though, I did not have time to feel lonely. He and I worked longer hours than before, and since he drove himself even harder than he had in the past, I stubbornly worked harder too, which was the only way I knew to earn his respect; and I wanted that more than anything. Well, that is not quite true—to be entirely honest, I wanted that magnificent body of his, but I felt sure that was never going to happen, and I was willing to settle for his respect.

To my surprise, he announced a few days later that he had hired not one but two extra hands to help out with the work. "We got two less mouths to feed these days," was all the explanation he offered. If I had entertained any illusions that this meant our work would be less as a result, they were quickly dashed. If anything, we just worked still harder.

I saw right off the bat that he took care to keep me well separated from those hired hands, which made me wonder if he had guessed that I was the same as Win. I was not about to make the same mistake as Win had made, however, and I avoided those two men like the plague. Anyway, whether it was by chance or by design, I could not say, but he had surely picked the two most unattractive men in all of Rawley's Landing. Maybe in all of Kentucky.

With the extra help, though, the backfield was cleared of trees at last, even the stumps were dug up, and the field leveled off, and ready for planting. The fence was done as well, and from somewhere Branston acquired a small flock of sheep, only twenty of them to begin, but it was a start, at least.

He let the hired hands go then, and I breathed a deep sigh of relief. I had not the slightest interest in any sort of sexual adventure with either of them, but it was a strain to feel that Branston was constantly watching for any sign of trouble. I was almost tempted to tell him whose dick it was that I was aching for, but I had a notion that I would not improve relations any between us by telling him that.

* * * * * * *

It was not long after we had gotten the work all caught up, and things did actually become a little easier for us, that Branston surprised me one evening with some news. It seems that we were going to make a trip to a city called Paducah.

"For the regatta," was how he explained it.

I did not know what that was, a regatta, but I kept my ignorance to myself. Anyway, I did not much care. Just knowing that we would be going on a trip, the two of us, was exciting enough for me.

"Everyone puts on this big pretense, that regatta week is nothing but a social do," he explained over the dinner table that evening, "But what it really is, is people get together and work out all sorts of business matters over a julep or two. I have got to raise us some money, and that will be the best time and place to do it. And I reckon you might learn a thing or two yourself while you are there." Which answered the question that I had been fretting about—I was definitely going with him.

"It is just too bad that you could not take him to the derby," Leticia said, but I could see she was as excited by the news as I was. "The Kentucky Derby," she explained, turning to me. "Which is just about the most important horse race in the entire world, and people come from all around the world to see it. It is like Christmas and New Years and Mardi Gras, all put together, and everyone dances in the streets and has themselves the biggest old party."

"Party is exactly what it is, unfortunately," Branston said. "Everyone is too busy getting drunk and betting on the horses to do any business there. We don't have the time or the money to waste on that sort of nonsense. Regatta week is better, for our purposes, anyway."

"Well, the regatta is lovely, too, of course," Leticia opined and, apparently divining my ignorance, added in my direction, "It's a boat race, on the river."

"The Cumberland River?" I asked.

"Oh, my no, this is on the Mighty Ohio," she said. "The Governor's Cup, it is called, and the very cream of society, the old guard, as they fancy themselves, they are all there, all turned out in their Sunday best. We have always been, too, except for the last year or two when we, well, we just couldn't manage it." She looked imploringly down the table Branston's. "Will I be going too, Bran?" she asked in a hopeful tone. "Oh, do tell me I can go."

"The ladies will be expecting you, I imagine," he said, and for once his manner toward his mother was far softer than it often was, downright friendly, even. Whether it was that, or the news that she would be accompanying us, Leticia was downright giddy with the excitement of getting ready.

The old flight bag in which I had brought my few belongings here from Greece clearly would not serve for our trip to Paducah, where it seemed we were to put our best foot forward. The next morning Branston brought a shiny leather suitcase, not new, but elegant and well cared for, to my room.

"This is for you, to pack your things in for the trip to Paducah," he said. I almost ran to hug him in gratitude, but luckily I caught myself in time. He did not notice, of course. "It's just gathering dust in the attic."

I had no idea how to pack it, unfortunately. That old flight bag was all I had ever had, and finally had to confess my ignorance to Leticia, but she was delighted to help me with it, and I carried it proudly downstairs on the morning when we were to leave, hardly any less excited than she was.

Even more exciting, for the very first time I got to ride in that big black Caddy that sat in the barn. Branston had waxed it and polished it till you could see your image in the fenders like they were mirrors. At his direction, I settled into the front seat beside him, with Leticia in the back. I had never dreamed of anything so comfortable or luxurious. It seemed like there were acres of room inside the car, and the only sound was the faint whisper of the air conditioning. When we were on the highway, on our way, it felt as if I were floating on a cloud.

Of course, Branston drove as skillfully as he did everything else, and he was in a talkative mood, at least for him. "We will be coming in here regularly as the summer winds down," he said as we neared Paducah. It had taken not much more than an hour to get there. "Paducah is a big tobacco market. But that is not what we are selling today. We will be selling the Rawley name today, in a manner of speaking."

"Goodness gracious, look how things have changed, Branston," Leticia exclaimed from the back seat. She sat forward and leaned to the window to peer out, and I looked too, although the city was entirely new to me. "Look there, all those pretty motels everywhere. They were none of them here the last time we were in Paducah, I swear they weren't. And right here along the highway, too, isn't that something? And there, that one has even got a swimming pool in front of it, of all things. Can you imagine that, swimming in a pool, and right out here where everyone driving by can see you?"

"We won't be needing any swimming pools," Branston said. "Anyway, those places are there for the tourists. We will stay where we have always stayed."

"That is The Covington," Leticia told me, "The biggest and grandest hotel in town. Our family, the Rawleys, have always stayed there, since it was built, I expect, a hundred years, maybe, or more even." Her voice grew wistful and a dreamy look came into her eyes. "At one time, they kept the entire top floor exclusively for us, the Rawleys, they never rented it to anybody else at all. We would arrive, and there would be bottles of bourbon waiting for us, for the men folks, and champagne for the ladies, and big old vases of flowers all over the place, you could just about swim in them, and everyone bowing and scraping all over the place and saying, 'yes, sir,' and 'yes, ma'am.' Even later on, when it got to where we could not always pay the bills anymore, the top floor was still saved for the Rawleys."

"That was all years ago," Branston said dryly. "Nowadays, we have to call ahead the same as everyone else and make a reservation. The woman I talked to when I called didn't even seem to know our name."

"Imagine that," Leticia said sadly. "Not knowing the Rawley name. At the Covington, of all places. How times have changed."

"They will know it again," Branston said firmly. "I mean to see to that."

I looked across the wide front seat at him. I had never seen him so mellow as he was on this occasion; nor as elegant, either. He wore a wide brimmed hat, a Panama, he called it, and a dark blue suit that fitted his splendid physique to perfection, with a crisp white shirt and a yellow silk tie; and his shiny boots were something he had called "alligator." There was none of the rough farmer about him now.

Leticia had said he looked every inch the country gentleman. I did not know about that, never having known any country gentlemen, but he was beyond any doubt the most beautiful man I had ever laid eyes on, and I had spent much of the trip staring in awe at him, but if he had noticed, or minded, he did not show it. Once, he had looked across the seat and actually smiled at me, a real smile, and not one of those nasty things he sometimes threw at others, and my heart had nearly stopped beating and I had to look away so he would not see how furiously it made me blush, like a silly school girl.

Leticia was in her best finery, too. She wore a flowery dress of some shimmering material that billowed about her legs as she walked, and big floppy hat with flowers all around it. She looked astonishingly young, almost beautiful again; I wondered how long it had been since she had been away from the farm and Rawley's Landing.

Leticia and I had packed my new suit as Branston instructed, but I wore my jacket and tie for the trip. It was clear that we were to put on a show for the cream of Paducah society, and I nervously prepared to play my part as best I could.

It was going on noon when we pulled up in front of our hotel, a big, classic looking building that reminded me of the Grand Bretagne, the famed hotel back in Athens. It looked elegant and genteel, and just a trifle run down. A black man in a purple and gray uniform came out to greet us. I followed their examples and waited for him to open the door before I climbed out.

Branston handed him the keys and said, "We will need us a driver for the day. See to it, will you."

"Yes, suh," he said, and smiled deferentially at us. I almost expected him to bow as we passed. It was one of those times when it really was a thrill to be a Rawley, even if only a poor relation.

* * * * * * *

I would like to have fantasized as to why Branston had arranged for him and me to share a bedroom, pretending that he had romantic notions, but of course I knew better: it was because it was cheaper than getting separate rooms. In any case, it made my blood run a little faster to know that I would be sharing it with him, that he would be sleeping in the bed next to mine that very night, only a few feet away from me. I felt certain that my dreams would be special ones indeed, and I prayed that they would not lead me to sleep-walk. I would not have minded, however, if he had done so. The welcome that awaited him in my bed was considerably warmer, I felt sure, than the one that I would find if I made my way to his.

Leticia had a bedroom of her own, of course, and between the two sleeping rooms was a living room of sorts—he called it a "sitting room." There were flowers in Leticia's room, not masses of them, the way she had described, but a beautiful arrangement of them in a tall vase, and another arrangement, not quite as splendid, in the sitting room, though none in ours. I wondered if the flowers were from the hotel, or if Branston had ordered them. Leticia seemed to think that it was the former, and if she was mistaken, Branston said nothing to correct the mistake.

I freshened up first, while Branston talked on the telephone, and I put on my suit, and sat in a chair to wait for Branston. He finished his conversation and went into the bathroom, and came out bare-chested a few minutes later, and put the white shirt on again. He took a small box out of his suitcase and tossed it to me.

"Put that on," he said. "And mind you be careful of it, it's worth a pretty penny.

I opened the box. There was a stickpin inside, glittering against a black velvet background.

"Why, this is…" I stammered.

"Yes. It's a diamond," he said. "A good one, as it happens. I was going to wear it myself, for show, but I think we need to fancy you up a bit. Put it in your tie, about here." He indicated where it went, looking oddly embarrassed and, without waiting for me to put it in my tie, went back into the bathroom.

I stood in front of the mirror over the dresser and stuck the pin in my tie with trembling fingers, and stared. The diamond must have been two carets, three even. The way our finances were, it represented a considerable amount of money, and I was astonished and touched that he would trust me with it.

"I guess you realize," he said through the open door, "We will pretend that we are here strictly for pleasure, the same as everyone else does, but this is really a business trip for us."

"I understand, sir," I said. There was a moment of silence and then I heard him peeing noisily into the toilet bowl. I had to make an effort not to walk to the door where I could watch him.

He finished and washed his hands, and came back to the bedroom, zipping up his fly. I forced myself not to look in that direction. "You're family," he said, in a not unfriendly tone, "Which means you have seen and heard things that I would not have let an outsider see and hear. But it also means I expect you to do your duty same as the rest of us."

"Yes, sir," I said. "I will do the best I can."

He nodded. "I imagine you will," he said. "You generally do, it seems to me." He poured himself a glass of bourbon and tilted the bottle in my direction, but I shook my head. I wanted to keep my wits about me on this very special day. Besides, I was already a little drunk on the compliment he had just paid me.

"The truth is, we are poorer now than a lot of common folk," he said, putting the bottle back on the dresser and half-emptying his glass. "But we have still got the Rawley name, and believe it or not, that is still worth something. It is here, anyway, which is why I have tried so hard to keep some things from becoming public knowledge. We have got the farm, too, even if we do owe money on it. We have cut back on expenses, and if I can boost our crops a bit, now that the two of us have got that extra land cleared—if I haven't said so, I appreciate how hard you have worked to help me with that—well, what I mean to say is, I reckon we can be back on our feet in a year, two at the most."

120

I did not know exactly why he was bothering to tell me all this, but I listened in respectful silence, flattered by the camaraderie, and delighted with the praise, however off hand it might be.

"That is why we are here, then," he said. "I need to raise us some money, to pay off some of those old debts, and to finance the increased planting we will do next season. There's people here who still look up to the Rawleys, and some of them have money. Our job is to convince them to hand it over to us. It's ass-kissing, is what it comes down to, but in a gentlemanly fashion, which makes it agreeable to everyone concerned."

He paused and looked directly at me as if he too wondered why he was telling me all this.

"Well," he finished, emptying his glass, "What I am trying to say is, you are a Rawley now, even if you do have a funny name. Be careful you don't let anything slip about how lean things have been for us, and we do not need to be telling any tales about Ellen or Win, either. Do you understand me, boy?"

"You do not need to worry, I will not say anything," I promised.

"Good boy." He looked at me long and hard for a moment, up and down. It was impossible for me to guess what was going on behind those amethyst eyes. Finally, he went to the closet and got his suit coat, and slipped into it. "Well, I do not mean to suggest for a moment that you are not going to enjoy yourself while we are here. I am sure you will," he said. "Just now, we have got ourselves a burgoo waiting for us."

"A..." I could not get the unfamiliar word out. "A...what do you call it, sir?"

He grinned a really beautiful grin then, wide and showing splendid white teeth. "A burgoo. That will be something for you to remember, boy, your first one. A burgoo is, well, let me see, it is a lot of different things. It's a party, to start, or more like a cookout, since it is always held out of doors, and they serve a stew, which is also called a burgoo, and that has got chicken in it, and some squirrel as a rule, and, well, all kinds of good things, you'll see. Let's go fetch Leticia. I expect she is still fussing with her hair."

He was right about that, but she finished getting ready quickly once Branston came for her, and it was only a few minutes later before we were going out the front door again. The Caddy pulled up for us exactly on cue as we came out, a black skinned man in a dark uniform behind the wheel. He jumped out and opened the door for us and we all three got in the back. There were little fold down seats that faced backward and Branston took one of those so that he was facing Leticia and me as we drove.

It seemed funny to me, his driving us here from the farm and then hiring someone else to drive us to this burgoo, but that apparently was how the Rawleys did things when they were in the city. In any event, I was not much inclined to complain, since he was sitting directly in front of me and that little fold-down seat was low, with the result that his long legs were spread wide, on either side of mine, and his well filled crotch where I could hardly help looking at it. Which soon caused me a problem, since my crotch was where he could easily see it too, and it had begun to swell. I tore my eyes away from that splendid view and looked out the window instead. Interesting, if nowhere near as special.

Paducah was not, so far as I could tell, a large city, but it looked old and it was pretty, and quite thrilling to me after the months on our farm. We left the commercial district behind, and drove through a rather elegant residential neighborhood. The houses got bigger, the properties more wide spaced and, finally, after a ways, we turned into a long, sweeping drive.

"This is the Handelson's place," Leticia said, leaning toward her window and positively bubbling over with her excitement. "My, I can not think when I last saw Melody Handelson. It has been years, I guess."

"She will be just as silly as she ever was," Branston said, but in a not-unkindly tone of voice. "I think you can count on that."

The house came into view, a house similar in design to ours, but smaller. The drive was parked thick with cars that spilled onto the grass as well, and the lawns teemed with well-dressed people milling about. Faint in the distance, I saw a glimmer of sunlight on water. "Is that the river?" I asked.

"Yes, that is the Ohio," Branston said.

"Will we watch the race from here? The regatta, I mean."

"That's for tomorrow," Branston said, "And we will be over to the Carroll's for that. Today is the day everyone sizes up everybody else."

"The Carroll's party is the event," Leticia said. "Everyone hopes to be invited to that, but not everyone makes it. Of course, we have a standing invitation. That is just understood."

I saw a row of fires burning and dark-skinned women in white dresses stirring the big cooking pots hanging over them. "Look," I said, pointing.

Branston laid one of his mammoth hands on my knee and squeezed it lightly. "That's the burgoos boiling," he said, "Just waiting for a little Greek boy to come along and have himself his first taste. I hope your tongue is ready."

"I am looking forward to tasting it," I said hoarsely. I was boiling myself with that hand on my knee. He took it away a minute later, quite unconscious of what he had done, but it was not burgoo I was wishing now that I could taste; and my tongue was certainly ready. So was everything else.

THE GREEK BOY, BY VICTOR J. BANIS

◎ **CHAPTER NINE** ◎
▲

The house and the grounds were a kaleidoscope of people and movement, an ever-changing mass of color and confusion. I had not seen so many people since I had boarded the bus in New York City—women and men and children all chattering at once, and the air was a heady blend of flowers and perfumes, cigars and the spicy smell of the burgoo cooking across the lawn, carried with the smoke on the gentle breeze. There was a small orchestra seated in a gazebo, playing a waltz enthusiastically, though no one danced on the little floor before them.

Leticia was immediately engulfed in a sea of chattering women, all in their finery, and all obviously delighted to greet her. A crowd of well-dressed gentlemen quickly surrounded Branston as well, shaking hands and slapping his back, but always respectful, each of them waiting for him to acknowledge them first before they spoke to him. I was proud to note that Branston was emphatic in introducing me to each and every one of the men as the youngest member of the Rawley family. He even managed to get Dimopolous right, though he still said Spiro with that "eye" sound; but for the moment I did not mind.

Anyway, I had too much else to soak in. It was obvious that this crowd represented the high society of the area, and we were obviously the highest of them. Of course, I was only a distant relative, without even the Rawley name, so I did not get the full treatment the way Branston and Leticia did, but nevertheless every one was careful to show me a proper respect, especially with Branston making it clear that he expected it for me. Quite clearly, what Branston expected, he got, at least where these people were concerned.

It really was a pleasure, too, to see Leticia, not as the haggard and driven creature that I had seen too much of up till now, but a radiant and lovely woman in her rightful element. She might be man-hungry and daft, but no one present played the role of grand dame with her instinctive flair, and I could not help admiring her as she circulated among the guests, nodding regally to some, and pausing to chat with others.

I was seeing a different Branston from what I was used to as well. At home, he was a super-macho farmer who worked hard enough for a dozen men and ruled our home and family like a tyrant, but here he was every bit the "country gentleman" Leticia had labeled him, but in his own utterly manly way, without any of the foppishness that I detected in some of the other men. Of course, he was the best-looking man there, which might have been written off simply as prejudice on my part, but I could quickly see that I was not the only one present who thought so. There were plenty of the ladies eyeing him hungrily. I might add, so did a few of the gentlemen, but if Branston noticed that, he pretended not to. It was quite discreet, in any case, but it was the sort of thing that I was attuned to, and I knew what some of those quick glances meant. There were the same kinds of glances I took at him when he was not aware, and I felt pretty sure they meant the same thing.

Needless to say, I was every bit as enchanted by this new Branston as I had been by the other one; indeed, the contrasts in the two sides to his personality only made him all the more attractive in my eyes.

After a time, Branston settled himself at a table off to one side with three other gentlemen and began to talk earnestly. I felt sure that he had begun conducting the business that had brought us here. I wandered off on my own, strolling around the splendid grounds of the estate. Even with the hundreds of people milling about, the lawns managed to look vast, though I knew from what Branston had told me that there were not any fields of tobacco here or land to be cleared, or livestock. The Handelsons made their money in retail selling.

"They are shopkeepers," Leticia had sniffed disdainfully when I had asked, but Branston had been quick to correct her.

"They are wealthy shopkeepers," he said, "With lots of money in their pockets, and we need to transfer a goodly amount of that to ours."

Well, I could certainly see all around me the evidence of money. The house was splendid. It was not as big or as grand as our own, though it was in better state, and the lawns behind the house stretched spaciously down to the wide, muddy river. Branston had informed me that the state of Illinois began across the river, and I went to have a look. A line of trees on the opposite bank marked the border, but otherwise it looked much like Kentucky. The river was busy with traffic, fishermen and sail-boaters and occasionally a good sized houseboat, decks filled with partying people, who waved and saluted me good naturedly with cans of beer. I waved back. A tall, athletic young man dived naked from the deck of one of the boats, skinny-dipping, and I savored the view briefly.

There were a number of buildings between the main house and the river. Some of them I recognized. I knew the guest cottage without anyone's prompting, but I never did understand what a springhouse was. There was garage, too, the size of a barn, big enough for a dozen or more cars.

I wandered idly for a while, and gradually worked my way back toward the party and a bar where white-jacketed servants were dispensing something called mint juleps in frosted silver tumblers. I took one and tried it. A bouquet of mint springs filled the top of the tumbler, so that you had to bury your nose in their fragrant leaves to take a sip of the julep. It was icy cold when I did, and sweet and minty, of course, and potent with bourbon. Branston had told me that any man could enjoy a julep, and a brave man might want two, but only a fool would risk a third one.

I was sipping my first one, and thinking I might best limit myself to one, when I realized that someone was staring at me from a little distance away. I looked back at a handsome young man only a few years older than I was. He was slim and dark-haired, and his gray eyes were filled with mischievous laughter. When he saw that I had noticed him, he smiled and winked, and I knew in an instant that he was one of my own kind. I paused where I was and took a little sandwich off a table next to me, and smiled briefly back at him, and waited for him to make his move.

I did not have long to wait. He drifted over to stand next to me, admiring the table of canapés. He took one of those little sandwiches for himself, and said, "You are the Greek boy, aren't you?"

I did not reply at once, but took a bite of the little sandwich instead and chewed it thoughtfully. It was filled with some kind of green cheese filling, delicious and insubstantial.

I was used to Branston calling me "boy," and I had gotten to where I did not mind it coming from him—I think, actually, that I rather liked the way he said it, there was a kind of an intimacy to it—but I was not altogether pleased at having this young man, who was hardly more than a year or two older than I was, calling me that. I gave him a frosty look, but his smile was so friendly, and so flirty, that I decided at once I was only being churlish.

"I am Spiro," I said. I stuffed the rest of the sandwich into my mouth and offered him my hand, wiping it first on the leg of my trousers.

"I'm Daniel Longfellow," he said, shaking my hand warmly and holding it a bit longer than courtesy required. He winked again and added, "I guess you could call me Greek, too, in a manner of speaking."

We grinned at one another. I knew that he was cruising me, and he was plenty good-looking, and I had been without any sexual outlet for a considerable time now, so I have to confess, I did feel a twinge in my trousers.

I was fully mindful, though, of what Branston had said, about staying on my best behavior, and I was determined that I would not let him down. I let that suggestive comment go unanswered. Maybe another time, I thought regretfully, and tried not to notice the bulge that ran down the inside of Daniel's leg.

I glanced toward Branston then, and saw that he had gotten up from his table and was looking around. I thought he might be looking for me, and I gave Daniel Longfellow an apologetic smile, and said, "Excuse me, I will be back in a moment."

I started in Branston's direction, but I saw after all that he had stopped to speak to someone else, and I paused, not wanting to interrupt what might be an important business conversation.

"See you later, I hope," Daniel said. He passed close behind me and moved gracefully through the crowd, smiling and greeting a few as he went. His hand had brushed across my bottom as he passed me, and it was not until a moment later that I realized it had not been simply a flirtatious gesture—he had slipped something into my pocket.

I waited a discreet few minutes before I reached my hand into my pocket and took out a folded sheet of paper. "Meet me in the garage," it read, "And I will introduce you to a real long fellow." He had boldly underlined the last two words.

I grinned despite myself. Another time, I thought, I would have been quick to take him up on the obvious invitation. But I looked in Branston's direction again just at that moment, and at the sight of him, so beautiful to see, a truth popped into my mind, so sudden and so unexpected that it took me a moment to grasp it.

It was Branston that I wanted. I had known that all along, of course, since the first moment I had set eyes on him. What was new to me was the discovery that I wanted no one else in his place. I realized in that instant that no other man, regardless of how attractive he might be, could ever substitute for him.

I had always felt that the more men I had fun with, the better, and had never felt a sense of exclusivity toward any one of them. This was a feeling so new to me that my mouth fell open and I could only stare stupidly across the lawn at the object of my unrequited love. The very sight of him took my breath away. Not only my unrequited love, either, but my hopeless love. He was certainly that. It was impossible to think that he would ever be mine—but, hopeless or not, I knew I was bound by it. Even if the circumstances had been different, Daniel Longfellow would not be a suitable substitute. I greatly feared no man would be.

I looked after Daniel, meaning to give him a shake of my head so he would not waste his time making a trip to the garages, but he had disappeared from sight.

I hesitated, wondering what I should do next. It was pointless to even think now of having any kind of sexual relations with Daniel, even if that had not been too dangerous to contemplate in the first place, but I could not very well leave him to wait in the garage for something that was not going to happen. It would only take me a minute, after all, to find him and give him some sort of excuse. I could hardly tell him the truth, but I would think of something to say. Anyway, I had certainly admitted, if only tacitly, to my own homosexuality. If I just stood him up now, he was surely bound to be angry, and there was no telling what he might say out of spite, that might get back to the wrong ears. It was better, I thought, to try at least to cut things off in a friendly manner. I made my way slowly and discreetly through the afternoon crowd, in the direction of the garage.

I could see why he had chosen the garage for his planned assignation. The car doors were in the front, of course, but the walk in door was to the rear, away from the lawn and the curious eyes of anyone who might glance in this direction. No one would see who went in and out this way.

I opened the door and hesitated in the opening. It was dark inside, the more so in contrast to the bright sunlight outside, and for the moment I could see nothing. "Daniel?" I said in a whisper.

"Here," he said, appearing suddenly out of the shadows directly in front of me. "Quick, come in and close the door before anyone sees you."

I stepped inside and he quickly closed the door after me. He took my arm in a firm grip and led me further into the darkness.

130

"I just came to tell you, I cannot…" I said, and paused. My eyes were beginning to adjust to the gloom, and I saw to my surprise that we were not alone. Several shadowy figures moved forward out of the darkness. As I tried to make them out, they began to encircle us.

"Who are they?" I asked, puzzled, but not yet frightened.

"My friends," he said, and his voice had changed oddly. It was no longer friendly and flirtatious the way it had been before. It had turned cold and hard. "We want to talk some business with you, Greek boy."

"Business? What kind of business," I asked, but I had already begun to suspect where this was leading. I tried to back toward the door, and found that someone was directly behind me. I bumped into him in the darkness and he gave me a little shove forward again.

"Well, it seems we are all of us just poor relations, not a red cent between us," Daniel said, "But, take you, now, you are one of the Rawleys, even if you do have a funny sounding name, and everyone knows that the Rawleys have more money than God. Ain't that right, Chester?"

The one behind me giggled in the darkness and a different voice off to my left said, "That is surely so, Daniel."

I tried to laugh, to break the tension that was rapidly building. "Maybe the Rawleys do," I said, "But I am a poor relation myself. I do not have a cent either."

"Now, you know," Daniel said, giving his head a shake, "I just find that hard to believe, boy. Why, old Branston, the way he was fawning all over you out there. And that suit you are wearing, I recognize that. I know for a fact that it cost a pretty penny, and it's brand new, ain't it? And that stick pin, why, I could get three, four hundred dollars for that, I reckon, at any pawnshop, and I will gladly take that from you as a down payment." He held his hand out toward me.

"And whatever you have got in your pockets," someone else said. "We will take that, too."

I took a deep breath and clenched my fists. I had been chopping wood all summer, which is a sure way to build up your muscles, and I felt sure I was strong enough to take on

131

one or two of them in a fair fight; but I could see now that there were at least five, and maybe six of them. Well, I was determined that they were not going to get anything off me without a struggle, and I would die before I would let them have Branston's stick pin.

"Sorry. I am not giving you anything," I said, and waited for them to make their move.

Miraculously, Branston called just then from outside, but not far away: "Spiro. Where did you get to, boy?"

"Bran," I shouted as loud as I could, "In here, in the garage."

Daniel took a quick step toward me. I ducked his out-stretched hands, but I stepped right into someone else's arms. I took a hard swing, pretending that I had my axe in my hands, and hit him in the stomach. He grunted loudly and fell back, but in an instant there were three others on me, trying to drag me between a couple of parked cars. I fought for all I was worth, and a minute later, the door flew open, light spilling inside, and Bran was there.

They scattered, but not fast enough. Branston caught one of them and sent him crashing like a rag doll across the hood of a car. Daniel had picked up a tire iron from some-where and swung it at Branston, but Branston knocked it out of his hand like it was a toothpick and threw him against a wall. The others fled like rats, scrambling over one another to get out the door.

To my surprise, Daniel stayed. "My arm," he said, cradling it, "I think you broke it."

"I ought to break your neck, you little bastard," Branston said, taking a menacing step toward him, but Daniel managed to stand his ground.

"Go ahead," he said, "But maybe first you had better ask your little Greek boy what he is doing here in the garage in the first place. He was ogling my dick outside, that's what he came here for. Or didn't you know he was a little cock-sucker?"

Branston turned on me, astonished and accusing. I had not come here to suck Daniel's cock, but it must have seemed to Daniel like I had, since that was why he had in-vited m to begin with. Anyway, the other part of it was certainly true enough: I was a cocksucker, even if that was not exactly the term I would have used.

But I was flustered at having Branston find out like this, and though I wanted to tell him the truth of why I was there, I knew I could not help but look guilty, for having hidden the truth about myself from him for so long.

"Bran," I started to say, but he had already seen the truth in my face, or enough of it at least to convince him of the rest. He grabbed hold of my arm and all but dragged me out of the garage. Behind us I heard Daniel laugh cruelly.

"Go up to the car," Branston said, and when I tried to speak, to explain to him why I really had gone to the garage, he said, sharply, "Not a word. Do as I tell you."

He went quickly up the hill, steering a path through the crowds of party guests and ignoring everyone who tried to speak to him. I followed in his wake, almost running to keep up with his long, swift strides.

Leticia was miraculously alone for a moment. "We're leaving," he told her. She took one look at his face, and at me, trailing forlornly after him, and set her glass of iced tea down and hurriedly followed us.

Our driver was napping behind the wheel of the Caddy and he almost fell out when Branston threw the door open. Branston thrust a wad of bills at him and said, "Here, take a cab back to town, I will drive us now, and thank you for your trouble."

Leticia caught up with him breathlessly. "Branston, what is it, what has happened?" she asked, but he only ordered her to get into the car. I climbed in after her, in the back seat this time, and before the door had hardly closed we were roaring down the long, winding driveway and were on our way back into Paducah.

Leticia was too frightened by Branston's obvious fury to ask any questions, though she shot me a puzzled look from time to time. As for me, I only sat huddled miserably in one corner of the back seat and wished I were dead.

A startled doorman took the car from us at the hotel and stared as Leticia and I rushed through the lobby after Branston. "Get packed," he ordered the moment we entered our suite.

Leticia went wordlessly to her room and I did the same. I stripped off my suit and, naked, began to pack it carefully into the suitcase. Branston had stayed behind in the sitting room to pour himself a glass of bourbon.

I was trying to remember exactly how Leticia had folded the suit to make it fit when he came into the bedroom; I stole a quick glance at him. He looked like he might have finished the whole bottle of bourbon in those few minutes. His hair was tousled and his eyes were those of a wild man. He had taken off his jacket and tie, and as he came into the bedroom he stripped off his shirt as well and tossed it aside, baring that splendid broad chest. He unfastened his belt and began to take off his trousers. Normally that would have filled me with delight, but I was so ashamed and scared that I barely noticed. I could only think about how I could possibly undo what had happened.

"You, dammit," he said, stepping free of his trousers. "I honestly believed you had some sense about you, that you were different from the rest of them, but you are just like every other Rawley, aren't you, man and woman, can't a one of you think of anything but cock. Jesus, why did you have to go sniffing around for it, there, today, of all the times? With that Daniel Longfellow, yet, I could have told you he was nothing but trouble, if I had known that was what you were up to."

I wanted to explain to him that I had not gone to the garage for that reason, but the words would not come. I was sure he would not believe me, and why should he? Daniel had not lied about that part of it, anyway: I was guilty, if only of eyeing his dick in the first place and giving him reason to think I was going to suck it when I got to the garage. In that sense, at least, Branston was right, I was not any better than Win or Ellen or Leticia, even if it was his cock and his only that I wanted now; but I could not very well tell him that, not here, certainly, and not now.

I had forgotten completely that I was naked until his angry eyes went up and down my bare body, and I shivered. "Shit, if you needed it that bad, damn you, why didn't you just tell me?" he said. "If that is all it would have taken to keep you out of trouble today, I would have fucked you myself, same as I did with Ellen. I got enough to go around, you ought to know that, boy, the way you been drooling over it."

He came toward me suddenly, grabbing violent hold of me, and forced me back upon the bed. I tried to resist, but I was no match for him and my heart was not in it. He pinned me down with his knees on my arms and his prick, growing bigger and harder by the second, right in front of my face.

"Here, by Christ," he said, "You need cock, well, here it is. Suck it, eat your fill of it, you can have all you want, I got plenty."

Since the first moment I had laid eyes on him, I had dreamed of this, had imagined it a thousand times or more, him kneeling over me, those big hairy balls swaying pendulously and that magnificent prick in my face. Its ruby head, dew bedecked, was no more than an inch or two from my lips, so close I could breathe in the raw man-smell of him. My arms were numb from his weight and there was a roaring in my ears.

"Suck it," he snarled in a hoarse voice. I did not need to be told again. I lifted my head slightly and took him in my mouth. It tasted clean and fresh and sweeter than any cock I had ever known before, as I had known all along that it would. He seemed to grow even bigger and harder inside my mouth and it throbbed now in reply to my licking tongue.

He moved his knees, no longer crushing my arms with them, and took my head in his strong hands, pulling me toward him and thrusting his prick far down my throat. I heard him say, "Ah, god, god," like he was praying.

All of a sudden his cock was gone from my mouth. He moved back and, taking hold of my legs, flung them roughly over his shoulders, and moved forward again, bending me almost double. I heard him spit into his hand, and then I felt an unfamiliar probing at my virgin hole.

I wanted to cry, to beg him not to do this. I had longed for it, I had dreamed of it. I had saved that special treasure all these years just for him, for him alone, even long before I had ever met him. It was his, his and nobody else's. But not like this, I thought in anguish, not in anger, not uncaring; I wanted him to have it as a gift of my love.

I had no say in what was happening now, though. He had made up his mind to fuck me and fuck me he would. I was not strong enough to fight him off, even had I wanted to, and I knew I could never even have tried. He held me in an iron embrace, my legs over my head, and that huge knob of his broke through all resistance and forced its way into me.

"Bran," I started to say, I wanted to tell him at least that he was the first, that he was taking my cherry, but he thought I meant to protest, and he clamped a hand violently over my mouth.

"You'll take it and like it," he said, and I felt that tight channel surrendering to his pressure as he shoved it in. For the first time, I had the feel of a hard prick deep inside me. He rammed it in without pause, going steadily deeper, without a thought for the pain I was suffering. I resisted involuntarily, squirming beneath him and trying to pull away from him, but it was futile and it only fueled his anger and his passion.

"You wanted this, didn't you?" he demanded bitterly. "I've seen that little butt of yours twitching all the time. This is what you have been itching for, isn't it? Well, you have got it, haven't you?"

I stopped struggling and said nothing. I felt as if I were being split in two, and I was torn apart mentally, too. This was Branston's cock inside of me, and it should have been the happiest moment of my life; but he was not fucking me out of love or even out of desire, it was sheer hate that drove him deep into my bowels. I learned like others I am sure had learned before me, that love meant more than come.

For all that I was suffering, though, I still was aware that he was the most beautifully masculine man I had ever seen. That chest hovering over me, the arms that held me, the thighs pounding against my upturned buttocks were all as hard as if they were chiseled from rock, and though the pain that it caused me was agonizing, I still knew that the cock plowing in and out of me was the ultimate cock, a phallic symbol of love worthy of this god of a man, worthy of my worship.

His breath was a roar in my ears. Oddly, he gasped my name in a frenzied whisper: "Spiro. Ah, Spiro." I realized he was getting close to coming. He fucked me harder, and still harder, until I wondered how my mere mortal's body could withstand his assault, and at the same time, despite the pain, the heat of his passion was arousing me as well. My own cock had grown hard and was pressing between us, though I knew he was aware of it not at all.

This was a sexuality beyond reason, beyond sanity, even. For all the humiliation for all the agony, I looked up at those lips so near mine, and wished that I could kiss them; but I knew that would only make him even angrier.

He gave a final lunge, burying himself in me. I groaned despite myself. He seemed to grow even longer, to reach even deeper, and I realized it was his come exploding into the farthest reaches. The realization brought my own load shooting out of me, and I sobbed aloud and reached up with my arms to cling to his trembling shoulders.

Reality returned all too soon, however. He lay heavily upon me for only a moment before he moved, pulling out of me and standing quickly. I opened my eyes to look at him, and remembered with a shock his anger, that I had forgotten for a fleeting moment; and I saw something else, too, for just a second or so: an odd sadness and, strangest of all, a glimpse of confusion in his usually confident expression.

But it was gone in an instant, so quickly that I thought I must only have imagined it. He grabbed a corner of the rose-covered comforter on the bed and flipped it over me to cover my nakedness, and went wordlessly into the bathroom, closing the door firmly behind himself, and a moment later I heard the shower begin to run.

I rolled over onto my stomach and buried my face in the pillow to smother my sobs, and at last, I gave myself up to my tears.

THE GREEK BOY, BY VICTOR J. BANIS

◎ CHAPTER TEN ◎

It was a subdued trio that drove back to the farm later that day. I doubt that five words wore spoken among us the entire trip. I could not help remembering, when I finally got back to my room, with what eagerness and delight I had set out—had it really been that same day? It seemed as if an eternity must have passed since then.

It was quickly clear over the days that followed, that whatever friendship or sense of camaraderie had begun to grow between Branston and me was a thing of the past now We still worked closely together throughout most of each day, but that intimacy had been replaced by an icy silence that reigned between us.

I wished fervently that I could talk to him, could try to explain, but whenever I tried to start a conversation, he cut me off at once. He spoke to me only to give me instructions or to answer questions that were strictly concerned with our work.

I began to realize after a few days, though, that it was not just bitterness and resentment on his part. I saw that Branston seemed bewildered, even confused., and gradually I came to understand. He had worked so hard to restore our name and fortune, giving far more of himself than he demanded of anyone else, and he had believed that others could live without emotion or pleasure the same way he could. One

139

by one, everyone had betrayed him: Ellen, Leticia, Win; even me, however inadvertently.

I think I was the one whose betrayal, as he saw it, had hurt him the most. Certainly, I was the one who owed him the most, and he had every right to expect me to be loyal; and his disappointment in me seemed to have rocked him to his very foundations. He was suffering now, and I would have given anything to drain that poison from his spirit, to heal his wounds, but he would no longer let me get close.

I had one consolation, although it was a small one. Leticia told me that the business on which we had gone to Paducah had been concluded by the time we left. That, in fact, was why Branston had been looking for me when he found me in the garage. He had wanted to share the good news with me, to celebrate in a manner of speaking. I was glad to know, at least, that I had not sabotaged his intentions, but it only made my anguish that much more painful, to think of what it might have been like to share that happy moment with Branston, and to know now what I had missed.

Our abrupt departure from Paducah had shaken Leticia, too, and since our return home, she had behaved with a modesty and ladylike manner that ought to have given him some comfort, if he even noticed. I suppose in part she was afraid that, in his present morose state of mind, it would take very little to cause him to put her out of the house, and she was thinking of her own skin; but whatever the reason, she was a different woman.

Leticia's mental state had been fragile all along, however, and the stress of all these events was bound to take a toll on her. I realized that she was growing almost daily more vague and befuddled. She fidgeted much of the time and often, in the middle of a sentence, she forgot altogether what she had been about to say. At times I started to respond to some remark of hers, only to realize that she was not speaking to me at all, but to herself.

I found myself watching her anxiously. Branston was completely withdrawn within himself these days, more alone than I had ever known him, and if he noticed Leticia's increasingly distraught behavior, he gave no sign of it, but I grew more and more worried as the days passed, afraid of where this might lead.

Most alarming of all, I discovered that she had begun to roam about the dark house in the middle of the night, restlessly seeking some ghosts of her own creation. It was these nocturnal ramblings of hers that finally brought to a climax the emotional storms that had been building since we came back form Paducah.

Branston was at the heart of everything that happened here at our farm, needless to say. That was especially true of the bitterness that he carried within him. I had wondered often about this, without seeing what should have been all too obvious. Ellen and Win were relatives, of course, but the relationships were not close, and he could not have been emotionally very involved with either, despite his sexual liaison with Ellen. Leticia was his mother, though, and he could hardly not have emotional ties with her. Whatever it was from his past that had spawned the hate within him, I ought to have realized that it had to be somehow mixed up with Leticia.

If I had been a bit smarter or more sophisticated, I might have guessed the truth sooner, and maybe I could have headed off some of the trouble that finally came; but I was just a Greek boy in a new land, among people who were still largely strangers to me. I do not mean to say that I was just a witness to what was happening. Indeed, I had been playing my own part in events all along, but the truth is, I was largely unaware of my part even while I was playing it.

It was entirely by accident that I learned of Leticia's nighttime wandering. I had trouble sleeping one evening. The weather had turned hot, and there was not even enough breeze to stir the curtains at the French doors. I tossed and turned in my bed for what seemed an eternity before I finally decided I would go down to the kitchen and get myself a glass of milk. I did not know if there were any rules about raiding the refrigerator in the night, but to be safe, I avoided the creaky newel post and the banister, and left the lights out. There was moonlight enough to show my way, and I was careful not to make any noise to disturb Branston or Leticia.

I need not have worried about Leticia, as it turned out. I came into the darker shadows of the dining room and nearly collided with her. She was dressed in something white and billowy, and for a second or so I thought that I had met a ghost. I jumped back and gave a little gasp.

"Oh, it is you," I said, relieved, when I recognized her.

"Goodness," she exclaimed, looking as relieved as I was. "You scared me half to death, creeping up on me in the dark like that."

"Me, too," I said with a nervous laugh. "Sorry, I was trying to be quiet so as not to waken anybody."

"Well, you certainly made no noise," she said.

We stood there rather awkwardly for a moment. The way she regarded me made me nervous, thinking about the way she had attacked me before, and I said, "I was just going to get myself a glass of milk. I hope that is all right."

"I am sure no one would begrudge you that," she said.

There was something more about her, though, than the memory of her lasciviousness, that made me uneasy. She looked not quite herself. I almost wondered if she had been in Branston's bourbon, but it is hard to disguise the smell of that on your breath, and I detected nothing. "Can I get you a glass?" I asked.

"Of milk? No, thank you, thank you kindly, just the same. I think I will just slip back upstairs," she said. "After everything else that has happened, there is no telling how Branston would take to finding the two of us prowling around in the dark together. He is liable to get all kinds of ideas in his head. You know Branston."

"You are right, I guess," I said, "Though I doubt he would be as hard on you as he was on the others. You are his mother, after all."

She laughed softly, a funny, chilling kind of laugh. "You don't understand at all, do you?" she asked. "It's me that Branston hates most of all."

The moment she said it, I knew that it was true; I must have known it all along, without putting it into words in my mind. "But why?" I asked. "Why should he?"

142

I thought for a moment or two that she was not going to answer me. She turned from me and started to go from the room, seeming to fade into the darkness like that ghost I had mistaken her for earlier, but as she disappeared through the dining room door, she said without looking back, "I loved him too much."

She disappeared without another sound, so that I almost wondered if I had dreamed her, or if she had been a ghost after all; but the scent her perfume lingered after her, faint and too flowery sweet, to tell me she really had been there.

I got my milk without turning on any lights, and drank it slowly in the dark kitchen, and thought about that odd meeting I had just had with Leticia. I did not know what her comment meant, but I began to understand that Leticia was not well, and I found myself worrying about what that would mean to our already strained household.

After that, I listened at night for the faint, telltale sounds that meant she was prowling about in the house. I could hear the careful opening and closing of her door, and the whisper of her footsteps as she passed my room.

At first, I did nothing, not sure that it was my place to do anything. She was, after all, the mistress of the house and I was not much more than a glorified houseguest. But after several occurrences of this, I decided to follow her one night. It was not so much that I had any right to dictate her behavior. Mostly, I was concerned that she might fall in the dark or in some other way hurt herself.

I stole from my own room and trailed cautiously after her down the stairs, feeling guilty for spying on her and nevertheless worried for her safety. She went along the lower hallway, to the front door and went out. When I slipped out after her, I found her waltzing on the damp grass in the moonlight, dancing with her arms up as though she had them about a partner. She smiled up at her phantom beau and talked softly to him as she circled about the lawn. I felt embarrassed to be a witness to something so plainly private, I left her there and went inside, but I did not go straight back to my bed. I waited in the darkness of the library doorway until she came in and, leaving a trail of dewy footsteps, returned to her own room. Not until I heard her door close softly again did I follow her up the stairs.

It was not her alone that I was concerned about, though. I worried about how Branston would react if he learned about her nocturnal prowling. She was half mad, I saw that now, and I wondered how he would respond to this new problem. If I had been a bit more confident of his sympathy for her, I would probably have screwed up my courage enough to being the matter up with him, but, sadly, I was afraid of what he might do, and I let matters go on too long.

Of course, I ought to have known that almost nothing went on in that house that Branston was not aware of. Somehow he learned about her nightly perambulations without my having to tell him. For all I can say, he may have known about them all along, before I did, even.

She went by my door again the following night, but just after she had passed it, I heard her cough faintly. The weather had begun to turn cooler, and I decided that she had to be coaxed back to her own bedroom before she caught cold. I got out of bed and quickly pulled on a pair of jeans, and slipped out into the hall.

To my astonishment, Branston was already there. He, too, wore nothing but a pair of jeans. He glanced my way as my door opened, and motioned with a finger to his lips for me to be quiet. "Wait here," he said in a whisper as he went past me.

Leticia was standing at the head of the stairs, leaning against the newel post and coughing quietly into her hand. She seemed entirely unaware of either of us. He caught up to her and put an arm about her shoulders.

"Bran," she exclaimed, startled. "You scared the wits out of me."

"It's all right, Leticia," he said, in the sort of soothing tone of voice you might use with a child. "Don't be frightened. Let me take you back to your room."

He led her back down the hall toward her bedroom. Though they went right past me, within inches of me, Leticia gave no sign that she had even seen me. I saw as they went by that she was smiling up into his face, and it gave me a shock. The expression on her face was unmistakable. I knew

144

it all too well. It was the one she had worn when she tried that first day to seduce me, and it was turned now on her son.

"Yes," she said, "Take me to my bedroom. You will come with me, won't you Bran?"

He did not answer but she seemed satisfied with his silence. She clung to him and leaned her head against his strong chest and said, in a little girl's voice, "It has been so many years, my darling, you cannot imagine how I have longed for you. But I will make it up to you, all that lost time, I promise, Bran, it will be just like it was before for the two of us. We will be happy together again."

I do not think Branston had paid much attention to what she was saying, but he did finally seem to hear and to understand. He paused and took his arm from around her, and turned to face her directly. In the moonlight, staring down at her, he was suddenly no longer the stubborn, determined Branston, the strong-willed man I had known since I had come here. He looked like a young boy all at once, shy and frightened, and altogether unsure of himself.

"Leticia," he said in a confused voice.

"Oh, I know I am older now than I was then," she crooned, "But I am still lovely, you will see. My breasts are as firm as a young girl's. Here, see for yourself." She took one of his hands and put it on her breast. He seemed to be spellbound. His hand did not move, but he did not take it away either. He was utterly motionless, silent, staring at her with an expression on his face that looked to me, in the pale moonlight, like fear.

"Remember how you sucked my titties, darling," she went on, "And my thighs, they are still beautiful too, and firm. You used to kiss me there, and suck at my little love nest, remember? And then I sucked on you, oh, you were so hard and so sweet tasting, and big, even as young as you were, you were already enormous. When you put it into me, I told you then, you were bigger even than your Daddy was, and you no more than just a boy."

She moved against him, hugging him, and turned her face up to him for a kiss. I felt a wave of horror and revulsion.

"Oh, my darling boy," she said, clinging to him, "We have wasted so many years when we could have made one another happy. All those men I took inside myself, it was only you I wanted, all the time, you I was searching for, and now here we are, and we can be happy again at last. Oh, make love to me, Bran, I beg of you, make love to me like you used to do."

For a few seconds he remained under her spell, and I thought he really was going to kiss her. I looked away in disgust and moved to go back into my room, not wanting to see anymore. He must have seen the movement, though, and it seemed to break the spell she had cast over him, and he gave a horrified groan that stopped me and made me look again, in time to see him push her away, so violently that she fell against the wall.

"Oh, Lord, Leticia, not again, never again," he cried. "I beg you, let me go, set me free from this curse."

"Set you free? You didn't want to be set free then, as I remember" she said in a petulant voice, rubbing a sore arm gingerly.

"I did, Leticia," he said, his voice choking, "In the name of heaven, can't you see that? Why do you think I left, why did you think I ran away?"

"Liar!" She changed in an instant, from a wheedling would-be seductress to a furious harpy. "You loved it, Bran, the same as I did, you are a hypocrite to try to pretend otherwise. You think I do not know when a man is pleasuring himself? I know what you are thinking. Yes, it is true, I am a slut, I am any nasty thing you want to call me, but I am your mother, and you fucked me, and you loved it."

I think that he had forgotten I was there, but he raised his eyes slowly then and for the first time since he had gone past me before, he saw me standing in my doorway. He continued to stare at me as he spoke to her, so that it seemed as if he were speaking directly to me.

"I was just a boy, Leticia," he said. "I hadn't but just started jerking off, and I had never even seen a pussy before except in my imagination. It don't take much coaxing to get a boy's prick up. One look at a naked pussy is enough to get it hard, and once it is, it has a mind of its own. Even if it is

146

your own mother that is doing the coaxing, even if it is your mother's pussy that is making it hard. Yes, I fucked you, and afterward I was sick with shame and guilt and I hated you, and I hated myself even worse. I ran away because I could not bear to spend another day here, with the Rawleys. It wasn't just you, it was your Daddy, our Daddy, and your brothers, and every last one of them. Pussy and cock, that's all the Rawleys lived for, it's all they could think about, day and night, and it didn't matter whose or when or where or how, like a damned bunch of dogs in heat. I spent years of my life trying to get the Rawleys out of my mind, out of my blood, and one day I finally realized that I would have to come back here and face you if I was ever to set myself free. I wanted to forgive. I wanted to make the Rawleys something to take pride in again. I wanted to be able to take pride in myself."

He paused, and this time I was sure he was speaking to me. "Can you understand?" he asked, in a plaintive voice. "It has made me hard, it has made me mean. How could I ask anyone else to love me, when I could not bear myself? When I filled myself with shame and disgust?"

She seemed to have heard nothing that he said. She took a step toward him and reached for him with her hand. "It's all right, my darling," she said, coaxing again. "It will be just like it was; we will make one another so happy again."

He sighed, sounding infinitely weary, and turned away from her. ""You're sick, Leticia," he said. "Go to bed now. Please." He reached past her and shoved the door to her bedroom open.

"I'm sick?" she spat at him. She took hold of his arms and jerked him around to face her again. "Who are you to judge me? You call me sick. What about you, Bran? You don't even know what it means to want someone. You have never even felt real passion, you have never loved anyone in your whole life, have you?"

For a moment he looked blankly at her. Then he looked at me again, with a look I had never seen before in his eyes. For what seemed an eternity, we were all three of us frozen in place.

Then, suddenly, he pushed past her and strode quickly to me, hurrying as if he thought I would be frightened by what he was going to do, or maybe because he was so frightened himself. It was all so quick, I hardly realized what was coming, until he had seized me in his arms and then his lips were on mine, tentatively at first and then urgently, forcefully, bruising my mouth, his tongue seeking mine.

I do not have any words to describe what I felt in that moment. Everything had ceased to exist for me, everything but that mouth crushing mine, those strong arms holding me so tightly they drove the breath right out of me, and his name singing through my mind over and over. Bran, Bran, Bran....

He took his mouth away finally, and looked down into my face. "I swear to you by all that's holy, I have never kissed a man before," he said, his expression solemn. Then, he grinned, a shy grin that spread across his face, not just his mouth, but his eyes, his whole face. "But I wanted to, wanted it so badly," he said, "That first time I laid eyes on you. And I wish I had, now that I see how sweet it is."

I could not speak, could only grin stupidly back at him, and stretch up toward him for another kiss.

Heartless though it sounds, in the thrill of our discovery, we had both altogether forgotten Leticia, until she screamed all of a sudden. I do not know if it was the sight of us kissing, or if it was just that Branston had chosen me instead of her, or maybe just the realization of how truly alone she was; but whatever it was, she was horrified. She screamed again and turned and ran from us, down the hall toward the stairs.

"Leticia," Branston shouted, and ran after her. For a moment I was too stunned to move; then I ran too.

I never knew if she meant to throw herself down the stairs or if, in her crazed state of mind, she simply fell; but I had taken no more than a few steps when I heard the crash of splintering wood as that rotted newel post gave way. It was so old it went like tearing paper, and Leticia went with it. She shrieked once as she fell and I heard her tumbling down the stairs, over and over, until she reached the floor below with a loud thud.

148

◙ CHAPTER ELEVEN ◙

▲

By the time I got down the stairs, stepping carefully over broken wood, Branston was already there, kneeling over her.

"Is she...?" I asked, and could not say "dead."

"She's alive, but she's hurt bad. Lucky her neck isn't broken, but just about everything else seems to be," he said, and looked up at me. "We'll have to get her to the hospital in town."

"Tell me what to do," I said.

"Get a blanket," he said. "We'll make a stretcher out of it. A big, strong one. Get the one off my bed. I'll bring the pickup around."

I hurried to do as he told me, but I had to pause in his bedroom. The bedcovers were thrown back, and the rumpled sheet still held the impression of his body. I took a moment to lean down and bury my face in the sheet, and fill my nostrils with the smell of him that still permeated the sheet. I think I would know that scent anywhere. It was like no other man's smell, like an aphrodisiac to me.

I could not linger there, though. I grabbed the blanket, and I could see why he had said to get this one. It was heavier and coarser than the one on my bed, and would make a better stretcher. I hurried back to him and together we got her on to it. I was surprised at how gentle he could be, especially considering the scene that I had just witnessed up-stairs.

He had backed the pickup around to the bottom of the steps while I was gone, and had wrestled a mattress into the truck's bed. We put her on that, and he sent me back for more blankets to cover her.

"You stay back here, with her," he said. "If she comes around, keep her quiet."

I had barely clambered into the bed of the truck alongside Leticia before he started off, shooting down the lane and leaving a trail of dust in our wake.

I will never forget that ride through the night to Rawley's Landing. I do not think another man could have driven that truck so fast in the dark, over those country roads and gotten us there alive. That old pick up bounced and groaned and threatened time and again to fly into the ditch or turn over on us. I clung to the side with one hand and tried to hold Leticia steady with the other, and prayed my heart did not stop beating. We spun gravel as we finally skidded into the parking lot at the hospital in Rawley's Landing. He jumped down and ran inside, and I breathed again for the first time in half an hour.

I was still trying to get my breath back and wondering if my legs would really hold me up by the time Branston came back around the truck with two men in white uniforms and a stretcher.

* * * * * * *

It was early morning, the night sky beginning to fade to dawn, before the doctor came to tell us how she was. There were broken ribs, and a broken arm, and a concussion, and lots of bruises, but she was going to live. She was still unconscious, but stable. They were going to transfer her in an ambulance to the hospital in Louisville, where she could be given better treatment.

It would be days, of course, before we could bring her home and, satisfied that we had done all we could for the moment, Branston and I went back to the farm. Branston would have followed the ambulance to Louisville, but the doctor in charge insisted it was not necessary, that it would be a day at least before she was conscious enough to even to know that we were there. And of course, there was a farm to run, animals to be tended, chores that could not be neglected, and no one but us to do them.

We hardly spoke to one another on the way back to the farm. My head was fairly spinning just to think of what had happened between us earlier in the hallway and I was afraid to say anything about it. I was afraid that he would say he was sorry for kissing me, and I did not think my heart would withstand a shock like that. I think I believed that it had been nothing more on his part than some sort of reaction to the ugly scene between the two of them, and I thought sure that when he had time to consider it, he would be embarrassed by what he had done, and maybe even angry, with himself, if not with me.

Anyway, whatever had happened between the two of them, Leticia was his mother and she was badly hurt, and I thought it wisest not to intrude upon his thoughts. If there were anything he thought needed to be said, he would say it, and I vowed I would keep my mouth shut till I heard it. But that was as much cowardice as it was reason.

I went straight to my own room when we got home, while he put the truck away. It was already nearing dawn, the sky had turned a dusty gray, and soon enough we would have to think about the livestock, but for the moment I wanted just to get my wits back. I stripped off the jeans, which were still all that I wore, and threw myself wearily across my bed. And realized, finally, the full enormity of what had happened to me earlier.

Branston had kissed me, really kissed me, and he had not been drunk, and now that I thought about it, it did not seem to me that he had been out of his mind, either, or anything else that would explain it.

"I have never kissed a man before," he had said. How on earth was it possible, then, that he had kissed me, a homely little Greek boy?

I heard him come up the stairs, then, and his footsteps in the hall, and I held my breath. They stopped outside my door. He knocked, softly, and came in without waiting for a reply.

He closed the door after himself and stood for a moment looking ill at ease. I thought for a horrible few seconds that he had come to undo what he had done earlier, and my heart shrank.

"I guess I fucked things up," he said.

"What makes you say that?" I asked.

He strode to the doors that opened to the little balcony, and stood staring out at a sky faintly turning light. "We will have to get the cows milked shortly," he said. Which was certainly true, but they were hardly the words I was hoping to hear.

"I'm sorry," he said, without turning back to face me, "About that business out there, about Leticia and me. I wanted you to know. I wanted you to understand why I…it wasn't just her, of course, I didn't have to fuck her. But you know what they say: a stiff dick's got no conscience. Mine surely didn't. I have got no excuse, except to say what I said out there. I was just a kid and it all seemed to be just innocent silliness when it began, when she started fooling around, and by the time I realized what she was leading up to, well, I had this big stiff on. And I already knew about him, about her Daddy—our Daddy—poking her regular, hell, everybody knew about that, and I guess I thought, well, what the hell, what difference can it make if I get myself some of it? Only, afterward, of course, it did make a difference, a horrible difference. I was so sick I near puked my guts out remembering. I couldn't stand to think of her, couldn't even stand the thought of seeing her the next day. That's when I ran off, that very same night that it happened, I ran as far and as fast as I could get."

"Bran, you don't have to…" I started to say, but he waved me off.

"I want to," he said. "I want you to understand. You, if nobody else in the whole world does." He paused for a moment and I was afraid to say anything at all.

"I couldn't ever get away, though," he said. "I couldn't get away from myself. And I couldn't get this place, her, out of my blood. I stayed in touch, of course, I would swear I wasn't going to, and then I would write, to say where I was, and as soon as I did, she would write me back and beg me to come home.

"After a time, I saw that I would have to, someday, if I was ever going to put it all behind me. So when she wrote that last time and said Daddy had died, told me she was trying to run the farm, and they were near to losing it, that was when I came back. I said I would run things, but I would do them my way, and everybody else would do everything my way too. I thought I could make something out of the place, out of them. I guess I was a fool."

"You must not say that," I said hotly, sitting up on the bed and forgetting altogether that I was naked. "You have worked damned hard, and you have accomplished a lot. Why, in another year, or two at the most, you will have this place out of debt, I know you will. And I will help, Bran, I swear, I will do anything in my power to help you, I will never embarrass you again. I would sooner die."

He turned to look at me then, and grinned that heart-wrenching grin at me. "You," he said. "You come along out of the blue, and I looked at you getting out of the station wagon, the day you arrived, and I said to myself, oh, fuck, that little beauty is going to upset the apple cart for sure. I could see every one of them starting to get hot in the britches at the sight of you. Shit, I half got a hard on myself just looking at you, that very first day, standing at the bottom of those stairs, staring up at me, and looking like a scared puppy. Oh, Jesus, if you had only known how bad I wanted you in that minute. It was all I could do..." He stopped and shook his head.

"You?" I could not believe what I had just heard. "But I did not...you never...*you*?"

"Well, I am not what you would call a virgin when it comes to men, least not in every way, and you might as well know that. Oh, like I told you earlier, I never kissed one, not till you, and I never did anything myself. I mean, well, I always just let them suck me off, or I buttfucked them. I won't pretend I didn't take any pleasure in getting serviced. I just never counted it for much, and I never even thought of doing anything more than that with them, I swear it. I thought the rest of it was queer, and I felt pretty smug about the fact that I was not queer. Till you walked into my life, and all I could think of was…well, I saw that I wasn't much better than the rest of them, except maybe a little more particular, it took a pretty little Greek boy to get my nuts hot but when they did they just never could seem to cool down. That was all I could think about, day and night, was how I wanted you. Working out there next to you in the field, in the barn, sitting across the table from you. I couldn't stop imagining what it would be like, to hold you in my arms, to make love to you. You can't imagine how badly I wanted that."

I could not think what to say; this was all so new to me, and so unbelievable. Branston, wanting me, all this time? And I had never guessed, never had even a clue? What an idiot I had been, I thought.

"I wrote your mother a letter, just now," he said. "I'll take it in to town later to mail it. We will take it, I mean."

I was startled—and heartbroken—to hear about that letter. I knew what it meant, I was sure. He was sending me back, back to Greece. I would die to leave him now, after he had kissed me, after what he had just told me. How could I go?

"Leticia is going to need someone to take care of her when she comes home, " he said. "She is sick, you know that, sick in her head. But I won't have her put away. I couldn't do that. And anybody else, anybody that wasn't family, well, it wouldn't be any time at all before everybody around here knew, knew she was crazy. I asked your mother if she would come here and take care of things, run the house, and look after Leticia. To keep it in the family, at least."

"Then, I do not have to go?" I asked tentatively.

"Go where?" He looked genuinely astonished.

"Back to Greece. I thought you were sending me home."

"Home? This is your home." He was puzzled. "Shit, I thought I got things squared away between us, that's why I kissed you, so you would know how I…are you saying you don't want…you didn't like that, when I kissed you?"

154

"Like it? Oh, Bran," I cried. I jumped up from the bed and threw myself on him shamelessly, flinging my arms about him. "Oh, Bran," was all I could say, like a repeating toy, over and over while I cried against his massive chest. "Oh, Bran, Bran."

After a while, he put a hand gently under my chin and tilted my head up and kissed me, and it was even more wonderful than it had been the first time. Those enormous hands of his caressed my back, and went down to my cheeks, fondling them.

"Well, now," he said, "There are those cows waiting to be milked."

"Yes," I said, trying not to sound disappointed. He *was* a farmer, after all.

"Of course, I got something else needs milking pretty bad, too," he said and grinned. "I guess the cows would wait till we got that done."

"I'm sure they won't mind," I said, and grinned back at him. "I will explain to them, I promise."

He cupped my naked butt-cheeks in those powerful hands and squeezed them gently. "Seems to me, though, like you are going to have to put something on, or I am going to have to take something off. It doesn't seem to me like it's good manners, the way things are."

"I like the second idea lots better," I told him boldly.

"I am glad to see you being so agreeable," he said. "Bodes well for the future, seems to me."

He lowered me gently to the bed, but when I went to pull the covers up, he stopped my hand. "No," he said, "That's too pretty a sight for you to rob me of it. And I have waited far too long to savor it."

He reached to turn off the light, but I said, "No, I don't want to be robbed, either, I want to see you too."

"Not much to see," he mumbled, but I could tell he was pleased. He peeled his jeans down while I watched with adoring eyes, eating up his flat belly and the golden oasis that appeared below it, and then that beautiful cock, already stretching itself out toward me. His heavy balls swung free as he stepped out of his jeans and, splendidly naked, came to join me on the bed.

"You'll have to be patient with me," he said, taking me in his arms. "There's an awful lot I don't know."

"This will be our schoolroom," I said between kisses. In reality this was our second time together, but that incident in Paducah had been so tragically wrong that I reckoned this our initiation to one another, and I was determined to make it perfect. He was not drunk this time, and he was not angry. If anything, he was shy and even a little awkward at first, but as things took their course, he got over that quickly.

I took the initiative, slipping from his embrace and kissing my way downward, tonguing his chest and his big nipples, and down over the rippling muscles of his flat belly, down to those wiry strands of gold. I could smell his sex, his maleness, and my mouth watered at the sight of his prick, fully hard now; but for the moment I only flicked my tongue over the head, and down the incredible length of the shaft, as thick as a boy's wrist, until I reached the downy orbs beneath. I licked first one and then the other, and sucked them one at a time into my mouth, rolling them around gently and making him moan with pleasure.

Finally, I gave my attention to his stiff rod, tonguing its length again, back to its dew-capped head, licking that satin flesh, and the sensitive ridge at its base. He was impatient, though, and he thrust toward me, shoving it into my mouth, and I welcomed the invasion, sucking hungrily at it.

To my surprise, he changed his position, turning himself about. My cock was in front of his face, and so hard and throbbing it would have been impossible for him not to notice it. He did, too. He took hold of it and moved toward it slightly, and hesitated.

"I've never done this," he said, his voice almost shy.

"You do not have to," I said, "It is okay."

"No," he said emphatically, "I want to. If I am going to love you, boy, I am going to love all of you. It's just that I don't know...oh, hell, it's time I learned."

He took it in his mouth, held just the head of it for a moment like he was considering the taste, and then slid up and down on it tentatively. It was altogether evident that he had never done this before; his teeth scraped the shaft painfully, but I made no objection.

156

Anyway, it was brief. He took it out of his mouth and said, ruefully, "That will take some learning. I guess." Then, quickly, definitely, so I could not misunderstand, he added, "We have got years to practice in, though. I promise I will get better at it."

The rest of it he did mostly by hand, lovingly and quite skillfully, now and again pausing to run his tongue over the head, and once or twice he sucked it into his mouth again and went up and down on it. Already I could see that he was indeed getting better at it, which I thought boded well for the future.

Mostly, however, my attention was focused on that magnificent cock in my mouth, one of the biggest I had ever had, and certainly the most beautiful, with that fat hard column that looked carved from marble and an oversized knob which I already knew from experience had been designed by some lascivious god of love to serve as a battering ram for tight little butt holes. Just at this moment, though, it was far down my throat, my mouth and nostrils filled with the sweet-salt taste of it, and down covered balls grazing my chin with each increasingly forceful thrust.

Branston was bringing me all too quickly to my climax, a fact that he apparently recognized, because suddenly he took the head into his mouth again, just as I exploded. Most first-timers do not try that, and he did not manage it like a pro—he choked violently and a lot of what I was shooting ended up on his chin and on the bed sheet, but he swallowed as fast as he could and he stubbornly kept his mouth on it, sucking until he had drained it of even the last few droplets and my trembling prick had finished its spasms before he let it slide free and flop across his cheek.

"If you are going to fire off a flood like that every time," he said with a hoarse little chuckle, "I am surely going to have to learn to drink faster."

I giggled briefly, but I was too busy with my own considerable mouthful, and now that he had only his own orgasm to concentrate on, he went at it with a single-minded ferocity, shoving that awesome prick of his full length down my throat, and then pulling back until I had only the tip within my lips; and down again. A half a dozen of those mighty lunges was all it took and he exploded in my mouth like a fire-hose going off, my mouth and throat filled to over-flowing with a mighty river of his nectar—one blast, two, three…I lost count, more come than I had ever known any man to shoot, and I drank it down hungrily, deliriously un-til—it seemed hours later—it did finally stop shooting, though it shrank hardly at all when he was finished and stayed just as hard as it had been before.

"Whew," I said when I could get my breath. "Talk about floods!" I was proud, though, that I had not spilled a single drop; and I hoped he had noticed.

"Well," he said hesitantly after a moment, "If you're not too drenched, that river is far from dried up."

Which was music indeed to my ears. I swallowed that fabulous knob all over again, and he began again to suck on my cock, and if he still was not exactly an expert, he was definitely getting the hang of it and, I have to say, it was probably the most wonderful blow job I had ever had in my life, the occasional scrape of his teeth notwithstanding.

This time we came together and he found swallowing a second load much easier, in part I guess because it was not as big as the first one. I am happy to say, though, that his was entirely undiminished, as bountiful and every bit as delicious as the first had been.

He was still as big and hard, too, which led me to suspect that the river still was not dry; but maybe he thought we needed to get our breath back. He turned around and took me in his arms, and kissed me, long and tenderly, and rested my head on his chest. For a long while we were silent, mo-tionless, just enjoying the afterglow of perfect sex, and the pleasure of holding one another. He tousled my curly hair with his fingers.

"I never dreamed I could be this happy," he said, and there was nothing for it, I had to turn my head up and kiss him.

He took my hand and put it on his cock again. That godly instrument of joy was still every bit as big and hard as it had been before, with no indication that he had already fired off enough come to float a raft.

"That, what we did the other time," he said falteringly, "When I, you know, in Paducah...did you like it that way?"

"I think so," I said. "It hurts a bit, when it is your first time, but I think it is probably like you said about sucking, it just takes a little practice."

"Your first time?" He raised his head and gave me a surprised look. "Are you saying, you were cherry? You had never done it that way before?"

I shook my head. "No, I had done just about everything else, but, well, I was saving that, till the right man came along."

"Oh, fuck," he said, clapping his hand to his brow. "And I came along and just plain raped you. You must have hated me to hell and back for stealing that from you. Especially when you have been saving it for someone."

"Stealing it? Who do you think I was saving it for?" I said. "I meant it to be yours all along."

He kissed me again, more passionately than before, and reached down to fondle my backside, his hand finding its way to my opening and one finger gently prodding it.

"Do you think..." he said, stammering shyly. "If it wasn't too difficult, I wouldn't want to hurt you, ever...but, would you be willing to think about doing it that way again? Sometime, maybe?"

I took hold of his cock and it throbbed eagerly in my hand. "I always think, there is no time like the present," I said. I turned over on my side, my back to him. "Try it this way."

"I guess I had best remind you of something you might have forgotten," he said, moving up against me. "Us Rawleys never get our fill of fucking."

"You are forgetting something yourself," I said, "I am half Rawley."

"So you are, by God," he said happily. "And the right half, too."

His cockhead poked against my ass, but not where it would do him any good. I spit on my hand and reached behind me to rub his knob with it, and guided him to me. He let me work it in, holding him steady and wriggling my butt back against him, until I got that thick head past my tight little muscle and he was planted in me.

He took charge then, forcing it slowly deeper, his shaft entering too. It was painful at first, the tunnel too small and the invader too large, but he took his time, and reached around me to grab hold of my cock, stroking it fondly so that the pain in my butt quickly lessened and became instead a pleasure.

After a moment, he paused, and asked, "Am I hurting you?"

Hurting me? This was Branston, my beloved, inside me, filling me up, the two of us truly made into one. I groaned with a happiness I had never known before, and pushed back against him, welcoming the rest of him into me, and he buried it to the hilt.

"Damn it," I said, "Why do you not stop worrying and start fucking."

He did, too. Cautiously at first, and then more enthusiastically, he began to pump me, and I squirmed and shoved it hard back at him, to encourage him. He was fucking me furiously now, driving that horse cock home and pulling almost out, and then in again, all the way, his balls crushing against my thighs.

Suddenly, it was gone, his cock withdrawn completely. I opened my eyes, astonished, but before I could say anything, he had rolled me on to my back, and lifted my legs into the air.

"I want to see you," he said. "I want to look at that pretty little face while I fuck you."

I grinned up at him as his cock came home again to its rightful place, to what would always be its home. "I do not think it is so pretty," I said.

He kissed me, and lifted his head to look me up and down with glowing eyes. "It is, all of you is," he said, and began to fuck me harder than before, and jerk my eager cock at the same time. "Damn, boy, you are unbelievable, I never had my prick in anything so wonderful before, I'm going to come, I can't wait..."

His body trembled violently and I felt him erupt deep inside me, spasm after spasm, seemingly no less than he had poured down my throat before, and the feel of it spewing into me set my own climax off. Almost before I realized it was coming, I was shooting, great spurts of white, hot juice splashing over his hand and onto my belly.

He lay across me for a long time, still in me, and I felt that he was no softer or smaller than before. I was beginning to suspect that he was going to be a tireless lover. I certainly hoped so. We had a lifetime of days ahead of us to fill up.

As if I had spoken aloud, he said, "And to think, we're just getting started.

"I was just contemplating," I said, "A great number of things I will want to show you."

He kissed me again, and gave me a devilish grin, and astonishingly, gave my asshole a tentative poke with that horse-dick of his. "You know, I just might have a trick or two to teach you."

After a few minutes of silence, broken only by our increasingly ragged breathing and the creak and groan of the bed as he began to ride me again with no less enthusiasm than before, he said, into my ear, the sweetest words I had ever heard spoken: "I love you, boy."

* * * * * * *

Later, when we got our breath back again, and we had finally remembered those poor cows waiting in the barn, he asked me, "How do you say that name of yours, again? Speye-row?"

"Spear-row," I said with a sigh, slipping my shirt on.

"Surely is a funny name," he said. "I think I'll just go on calling you 'boy,' if that's all right with you."

"I think that is probably simplest," I said with a smile. I doubted that he was ever going to learn to say it right anyway. And besides, when he said, "I love you, boy," it was music to my ears.

Always has been.

◙ ABOUT THE AUTHOR ◙

Lecturer, former writing instructor, and early rabble-rouser for gay rights and freedom of the press, **VICTOR J. BANIS** *is the critically acclaimed author ("...a master storyteller"—* Publishers Weekly*) of more than 140 published novels and nonfiction works, and his verse and short pieces have appeared in numerous journals (*Blithe House Quarterly, *Fall 2006) and anthologies (*Charmed Lives, Lethe Press, *2006).*

162

Printed in the United Kingdom
by Lightning Source UK Ltd.
131597UK00001B/225/A